"The Weddings"

THE WEDDING
IN
LONDON

Patrick Amadasun

Second in the Series

**Next in the Series: b) Wedding in New York
c) Wedding in Paris**

US Paper Warehouse, Inc.
10990 Galen Place
Johns Creek, Georgia 30097
USA
intergrain@yahoo.com

The Wedding in London

ISBN: 979-8-5140498-2-0

Library of Congress – Registration No.: TX 8-908-865

Printed in the United States of America

Dedicated to all lovers of the world that have
respect for the old tradition of marriage.
It is a good thing!

Contents

Chapter 1:

House of Lord Astor

The city of London in Great Britain is a mix of old tradition and modern norms. London is still the largest city in the United Kingdom since the 17th Century. The city is known for its diversity and openness to all peoples from every part of the globe. One of the well-known facts of the city is its well-developed labyrinth of underground rail system which is so old that it was initially powered by Steam Trains. It is also a known fact that the city has been inhabited since 4000BC. London is also known for its numerous Beer Pubs where the inhabitants hang out and have jolly good times. It is the city with Big Ben Bell, even though, most visitors believe that the tower with the clock is called Big Ben, howbeit, it is factually termed Elizabeth Tower. This is the city with Black Cabs and where the Queen has to ask permission from the Lord Mayor of London before

Her Majesty can enter the city of London. It is the city that Lord Astor and his parents live. Specifically, they live in one of the wealthiest part of London which is known as Belgravia or the billionaires' suburb.

Number 1, Grosvenor Square, Mayfair in Belgravia, London is a magnificent edifice on five floors. The luxurious accommodation is the house of the young Lord Astor that he shares with his parents, the Baron and Baroness Astor. The Baron and Baroness also have another main house in a town known as Astor. Lord Astor is thirty seven years old and he is a debonair, sophisticated and extremely fine gentleman. He stands about six feet and three inches tall with lean, muscular and trained body. He has piercing blue eyes that many women find very attractive and walks assuredly as if he controls the universe. He works under his parent, Baron Astor, as an investment banker in a brokerage firm owned by their family. Forbes magazine has estimated that Baron Astor is worth about $2.3 billion, while Lord Astor is worth around $400 million.

At about 7.30am, the butler knocked on Lord Astor's door to make sure that he was up and getting ready for work.

Lord Astor went to the door and opened it. He said warmly: "Good morning, Hector. Yes, I am up."

Hector replied and said: "Good morning sir. Your suit, shirt, tire and shoes are ready. Do you want me to draw your bath?"

Lord Astor replied and said: "No, Hector. I do not need a bath this morning. I will take a shower, instead. Thank you."

The butler left and Lord Astor started getting ready for work. Forty-five minutes later, he went to his parents room to give them is normal morning greetings. He knocked on the door and was asked to come in.

Lord Astor said warmly: "Good morning parents! How are you all doing this morning?'

Baroness Astor answered affectionately: "Good morning son. Are you off to the office?"

Lord Astor replied and said: "Yes mom."

He continued as he addressed his dad: "Are you coming to the office today?"

Baron Astor responded tenderly: "Good morning son. No, I will not be in the office today. I am going with your mom to a charity event, then, back to the House of Lords for some important business."

The Baron was only a ceremonial Chairman of the company which is mainly run by an astute Managing Director and supported by Lord Astor.

Lord Astor said: "Ok, dad. See both of you later this evening."

He took his leave from his parents and exited the palatial building. His chauffeur was already waiting for him and opened the back passenger seat for him. They started driving towards Fleet Street where their office was located. Twenty minutes later, the chauffeur drove and parked in front of a fifty-five story building. The magnificent glass house was the headquarters for Astor Investments, Inc. The chauffeur got out and opened the door for Lord Astor. He got out and went into the building as he was being greeted by the security men. He took his private elevator to the 55th floor.

The security men and receptionist got up and greeted him: "Good morning, my Lord."

He answered and said curtly: "Good morning."

He went straight to his private office and was greeted by his secretary.

She said: "Good morning, sir."

Lord Astor responded and said: "Good morning, Denise." He went into his office and sat down. He looked at his calendar and noticed that his secretary has informed him of a meeting at 11.00am with the executives on certain acquisitions that the company was planning to effect quickly before competitors become aware of the deals.

Denise, his secretary, was at her desk thinking about her wedding which will take place in three weeks. She knows that her boss will not attend, but, hoped he will approve her request for leave for her wedding and honeymoon. She decided not to ask him now, but wait till after his meeting this afternoon to remind him again.

At 10.55am, Denise walked to her boss office and said: "Lord Astor, the executives are in the boardroom and the meeting is about to commence."

Lord Astor replied and said: "Thank you Denise. I am heading there now."

He left his office and went to the boardroom. Everyone was seated, including the Managing Director. They all greeted Lord Astor as he took his seat at the head of the table across from the Managing Director.

The Managing Director opened the meeting and said: "Good morning again, Lord Astor, and colleagues. We have two acquisitions that we must move on quickly. The first one is Agar Pharmaceuticals that have developed a drug that will permanently cure diabetes. Our inside source told us that this new drug could increase the company sales from the current $1.4 billion to over $4.7 billion annually. A must buy for the company. Secondly, Devin Computers has designed cybersecurity software that could raise the company sales from its current $200 million to over $1.6 billion. We must move quickly on both companies."

Lord Astor responded and asked curtly: "Is it our intention to acquire them now and later take it public?"

The Managing Director responded excitedly: "Yes. And once taken public, we could add close to $2.5 billion to our company's net worth! Such deals do not come often!"

Lord Astor responded and said: "What does legal says? Will this be considered inside trading?"

The Executive in charge of legal matters responded and said: "We have examined the deals and it is not considered inside trading. The reason being that these companies are private companies, and not public companies that will trigger such problem."

Lord Astor said eagerly: "Thank you. This is good. Do we have the cash to get these deals done?"

The Managing Director responded and said: "We have the resources with our bank support to make these deals go through!"

Lord Astor asked calmly: "What figure are we looking at for both deals?"

The Managing Director said: "With a total of $6.00 billion, $4.5 billion for the Pharmaceutical and $1.5 billion for the Computer Company, we can get the owners to sell!"

Lord Astor said enthusiastically: "Then, Let's do it!"

All the executives agreed that it was a great deal and should be done immediately. After more discussions and delegation of duties to various executives that will enable the deals, the meeting ended.

Lord Astor went back to his office thinking that he and his parents just got filthy rich. The Managing Director and other executives will be well compensated. He has plenty to discuss with his parents at dinner tonight! Then, his mind went to his current girlfriend, Lady Chelsea, who enjoys and indulges in kinky sex - including ropes, blindfolding, whips, garter belts, swings and others. He enjoys it, but, only gets involved in it to please her. He is not sure if Lady Chelsea will be his future bride! Who knows? He has a date with her tomorrow, Friday, and they will hang out through the weekend.

As he was relaxing in his office, his secretary, Denise walked in.

He was in a good mood. He asked: "Denise, what do you want?"

Denise replied and said: "My wedding is in three weeks, and I need your approval to take a week of my leave time during that period."

Lord Astor said: "Ok. Go and type it up and bring it to me for approval.'

Denise said: "Thank you, sir."

She left and typed the letter and brought two copies to her boss for approval. Lord Astor signed both of the letters and gave it to her. One was for her and the second copy was for personnel.

Lord Astor stayed back in his office and continued doing other brokerage activities. Then, Lady Chelsea called. He picked up the phone.

Lady Chelsea said ebulliently: "Hi my Lord! How is your day going?"

Lord Astor replied charmingly: "Very well. Thank you Chelsea! What are you doing?"

She replied: "I am having lunch with my girlfriend. Are you seeing me tonight?"

He replied and said: "No, my Lady. Tomorrow evening is our date! Did you forget?"

Lady Chelsea responded and said: "No. I just want to see you earlier! I have a trick for you."

He responded curiously: "What will that be?"

She replied cunningly: "When I see you, then, I will share!"

Lady Chelsea is a stunning beauty with red hair and green eyes – a combination that makes her beauty devilishly alluring. She is thirty-six years old and stands about five feet and eight inches tall, which will easily qualify her as a potential model material.

Lord Astor responded tenderly and said: "Ok. I can't wait to experience this new trick!"

She responded playfully and asked: "What makes you think that it is something that you have to experience?"

He said equally playful: "Because, I know you my Lady!"

She responded teasingly: "Aha! You know me. Right? Well, wait till you see this new trick. It is out of this world!"

Lord Astor understands Lady Chelsea, and knows that she loves pushing the limit of her sexuality. He deduced that this new trick must be some new sexual acts she must have read in a new sexual playbook or something she conjured from her imagination! He decided to humor her.

He said mischievously: "After dinner tomorrow, you will have the whole weekend to show me your new trick!"

Lady Chelsea said excitedly: "Ok. Are you picking me up from my apartment at Knightsbridge?"

He responded and said: "Yes. At about 6.00pm. Then, after dinner, we will go back to your place!"

She said: "Ok. Though, I would have preferred going to your apartment at Knightsbridge."

He said: "Let's do your place this weekend and my place next weekend."

She said: "Ok, see you tomorrow, handsome!"

They hung up the phone and Lord Astor continued doing some work. At about 4.45pm, he left his office after summoning his chauffeur to get the Rolls Royce ready. As he exited the building, the chauffeur came to the left back passenger side and opened the door for him. The chauffeur got in and started driving the silver-colored Rolls Royce towards Belgravia, London. They encountered some traffic on the way and did not get to One Grosvenor Square till nearly 6.00pm. As the door was opened by the butler, he gave him his greetings and proceeded directly to the main study where his dad and mom were sitting drinking evening tea. The excitement of the day was evidenced all over his face and he could hardly wait to share the great news with his parents.

As he sat down, he said exuberantly: "Good evening parents!"

Baron Astor looked at his son and knew something good was up. He said: "Good evening, son. You look excited. What do you have to say for yourself?"

Baroness Astor chipped in quixotically: "Good evening, son. Yes, I agree with your dad. You look unrealistically very lively!"

Lord Astor tried to evade the questions from his parents and said: "When is dinner? I am ravenous!"

The mom responded warmly: "Dinner is in one hour. You have plenty of time to tell us the good news and change for dinner!"

He responded vibrantly: "I am the new billionaire on the block!" Then, he started laughing.

His father looked at him calmly and said: "Stop kidding around and do away with the suspense!"

Lord Astor said: "Dad, I am not kidding around. We are about to add about $2.5 to 3.5 billion to our company's net worth. This translates to about $1.8 billion being added to your net worth and $1.2 billion being added to my net worth. In essence, you will now be worth $4.1 billion and I will be worth $1.6 billion!"

The dad sat up straight and became more interested realizing that his son was not kidding around.

Baron Astor said impatiently: "Could you please explain and give me the full details of what you are talking about?"

Lord Astor responded by narrating all the details of today's meeting with the executives at the boardroom with regards to the two acquisitions.

He continued animatedly: "This type of opportunity only comes once in a lifetime and we intend to jump on it!"

His Dad was very excited now and was laughing gleefully. He said: "Go and do whatever it takes to make this happen!"

His mom said happily: "This is good and I am happy for both of you. But, I need some grandchildren. Lloyd, you are not getting younger, when are you intending to get married?"

Lord Astor responded to her mom nicely: "Mother, please let us enjoy this moment. I will marry once I find the right girl that I am madly and crazily in love with!"

His mom continued unabashedly: "I thought Lady Chelsea was the right girl for you!"

He answered: "Not really! We are dating and having fun. I do not think we are at the level of marriage yet!"

His dad jumped in his defense and said: "My dear, let the boy be. When he is ready, he will inform us!"

Lord Astor said: "Thank you dad. Let me go and change and get ready for dinner. We will talk more at dinner."

He left and went upstairs to his room. He dressed in casual evening clothes and went downstairs for dinner. After dinner, he retired to his own quarters on the fifth floor. He watched some news on television and decided to go sleep at about 10.00pm.

It was Friday morning at about 7.30am and Lord Astor was woken up by the soft knocking on the door by his butler. He got up and opened the door.

Hector said: "Good morning Lord Astor. Should I run you a bath, and bring you some juice and breakfast.

Lord Astor said genially: "Good morning Hector. Yes, please run me a bath. And in twenty minutes, bring me apple juice and scones."

Hector responded and said amiably: "Yes, sir."

Lord Astor added and said: "Also, tell my chauffeur that he will not be driving me today. Tell him to pull out the Aston Martin for me. I have a date with Lady Chelsea this evening and I will be driving myself."

Hector said: "Yes, sir." Then, he went to run his bath and left to get his breakfast and inform the chauffeur of the directives.

Lord Astor finished his bath, ate breakfast, and went downstairs to the fourth floor to give his morning greetings to his parents. Then, He got into the navy blue Aston Martin and drove to work. He parked in the special reserved area for the company executives and took his private elevator upstairs. The security men and the receptionist greeted him and opened the door electronically with an electronic sensor key to allow him into his private office.

His secretary saw him come through the security glass door and stood up to greet him. She said tenderly: "Good morning Lord Astor. Hope you had a rested night!"

Lord Astor responded and said: "Good morning Denise. I did. Thank you."

She responded and said: "Thank you for the approval, yesterday!"

He responded and said: "You are welcome." Then, he went into his office.

He worked throughout the day in his office and at about 4.30pm he decided to put a call to Lady Chelsea.

Lady Chelsea picked up the phone and said: "Hello my special one! Are you on your way, darling?"

Lord Astor replied and said: "Not quite yet, my lovely one. I will be leaving my office in about thirty minutes and hoped to be at your apartment at 6.00pm. Are you ready?"

She replied and said: "I will be ready when you get here."

He responded and said: "Ok." They hung up the phone.

At about 5.15pm, Lord Astor left his office and got in his navy blue Aston Martin and drove towards Knightsbridge. At about 6.00pm he arrived at Lady Chelsea's apartment. He parked and went to the door. As he rang the bell, Lady Chelsea opened the door and was looking ravishingly beautiful in black long pants and green blouse with matching emerald earrings.

Lord Astor stepped close to her and kissed her. He said admiringly: "Lady Chelsea, you look stunning!"

Lady Chelsea responded enchantingly: "Thank you. You look very fine, my special one!"

He said: "Thank you. Let's go to dinner."

They got into the navy blue Aston Martin and drove towards the restaurant called 34 Mayfair in Knightsbridge. Fifteen minutes later, he parked in the car park. He got out and went to the front passenger seat to open the door for Lady Chelsea. They both walked into the restaurant hand-in-hand and were seated by the host in a very private suite. Lady Chelsea ordered a Fillet of Cod dinner and Lord Astor ordered a medium-done Angus Beef dinner. Also, a bottle of red wine was ordered for the table.

Lord Astor looked at Lady Chelsea and said adoringly: "My special girl! You looked smashing!"

Lady Chelsea replied provocatively: "Thank you, my special one. You look smashing too!"

Lord Astor knows that Lady Chelsea is simply gorgeous and a great catch for any fine gentleman. However, he does not understand why he is not crazily in love with her. He wondered if he was capable of falling in love. At the same time, their dinners arrived and they started eating.

Lady Chelsea said seductively: "The food is sexy and reminds me of when we are making love!"

He responded inquiringly: "What do you mean my Lady? Are you now equating dinner to love making?"

She examined him alluringly and said: "Yes, darling. It looks and taste sexy like us! It is unlike masturbation which is similar to procrastination. It is great fun, except that you later realize that you are only fucking yourself! Then, it is no longer fun! That is why I enjoy you fucking me!"

He laughed out loud. He also knows Lady Chelsea likes kinky stuff. In addition, everything she sees is equated with sex. He looked at her and said mockingly: "We are not making love! Let's enjoy our meal!"

She responded obsessively: "You do not understand, darling. This is the way I see it. You did not ask me about my new trick!"

He responded tenderly: "I do not need to ask. You will show me when I get to your place!"

She said amorously: "My special one, once I show you the trick, you will quickly propose to me!"

He looked at her nervously and said: "Interesting! I did not know that you were interested in marriage!"

Lady Chelsea was surprised and a little annoyed and said: "You know every girl wants to be married to her Prince Charming! And you are the one!"

Lord Astor was seriously apprehensive and said: "My Lady, let's see our love develops before we start talking marriage. Let's enjoy our dinner and have fun!"

She was astonished at the non-commitment of her date, but pretended that everything was okay. She said: "Ok. Let's do that."

They finished eating and drove to Lady Chelsea's apartment in Knightsbridge. He parked and both got out of the car and started kissing as they went into her apartment. She closed the door and pulled away from him and ran upstairs into the bedroom with Lord Astor chasing after her.

She said spicily: "Pull off all your clothes!"

He said: "Ok."

And he pulled off all his clothes and stood naked before her. She too undressed and stood naked before him.

She looked at his manhood and saw that it was enormous and turgid. She said: "Follow all my commands! Also, remember that lovemaking is similar to a machine! You need a good screw to fix it!"

He said: "Ok."

She continued: "Get in bed and lay on your back."

He said: "Ok. What are you doing?"

She responded wickedly: "Today, I am in control. Just keep quiet and follow my commands!"

She took a silk cloth and blind folded Lord Astor. Then, took some silk ropes and tied each of his hand to each bedpost. The, she started kissing him all over his body. After fifteen minutes, as Lord Astor was squirming in pleasure, she sat on him as he entered her. She increased her tempo for about an hour until he had multiple orgasms and was heard making loud noises.

He said with ecstatic pleasure: "Please stop my Lady. I am exhausted!"

Lady Chelsea got off from him and said: "Did you enjoy the new trick?"

He said exhaustedly: "Yes. I did. But I am wasted."

She untied the ropes and took his blindfold off and said: "Aha! I wore you down today. You always wear me down. Today, I won!"

He looked at her and said astonishingly: "Where did you learn that from?"

She laughed and said: "Ancient Chinese secret!"

Lord Astor laughed and said: "You will not reveal that to me? Right?"

She answered and said: "No! I will keep it a secret!"

They laid down together and went to sleep. They spent the weekend making love and dinning in, and watching movies.

Chapter 2:

Home of Lady Elizabeth Selsdon

Belgravia, London is a very wealthy suburb with elegant streets that are lined with terraced stucco townhomes, garden squares, beautiful parks, and upmarket hotels. There are various antique shops, stylish furniture stores, hip galleries, and jewelry boutiques that cater to the rich. The suburb is also the place to go for designer fashion, expensive dinning, high-class restaurants, and chic cafes. The suburb took its name from one of Duke of Westminster's subsidiary titles – the Viscount Belgrave. Most of the buildings in Belgravia were designed by famous architects – hence, the reason it is referred to as the "Billionaire suburb." Belgravia has numerous residences that include celebrities, like Ian Fleming, Sir Roger Moore (James Bond), Lords, politicians, corporate owners, bankers, international embassies, movie stars, and artists like Frederic Chopin, Andrew Lloyd Webber, and Wolfgang Amadeus Mozart who wrote his first symphony at the age of eight at 180 Ebury Street. It is within this suburb that the house of Baron Selsdon is located.

A palatial, massive, and luxurious home on Herbert Crescent, Belgravia, London, about 0.4 miles from Hyde Park is the home of Baron and Baroness Selsdon, parents of Lady Selsdon. Lady Selsdon is in her bedroom on the 5th floor getting ready for dinner. She is 35 years old, slim, with a full mane of very black hair, and stand about 5' 8" tall. She has one of the finest blue eyes you ever seen on a woman. Her movement, her gait, her mannerisms, and everything else about Lady Selsdon epitomize sensuality, gentility, elegance and voluptuousness. With such beauty, it has been surprising to her friends that she has not been swept off her feet by one of the fine noblemen in England. Behind those blue eyes, is one of the finest brains in London! She graduated top of her class in law and has been sought after by most large firms in London. She has spurned the advances of these firms, and, instead opted to be the Chief Legal Officer of his dad's Pharmaceutical Company – a company with assets over $1.2 billion.

At about 6.30pm on a Friday evening, Lady Selsdon's maid-in-waiting knocked on her door to announce that dinner was ready. She acknowledged her maid and went downstairs to the main level for dinner. As she came into the dining room, she saw that her sisters Jane and Olivia, were already seated, and her parents were about to be served.

Baroness Selsdon said warmly: "Good evening Elizabeth. You look beautiful as always! You are running a little late for dinner. Are you ok?"

Lady Selsdon replied affectionately: "Good evening mother, and father! Good evening Jane and Olivia. Sorry I was running late. I came in late from my job."

Baron Selsdon responded tenderly: "Good evening daughter. Sit down and let's eat. We are all starved!"

Jane said: "Hi big sister! After dinner, Olivia and I are coming to your room to talk rubbish!"

Olivia said excitedly: "Good evening Beth! Yes, we are going to be in your room for girls talk!"

Lady Selsdon said enthusiastically: "Ok, sisters!"

They started eating dinner which comprises of Yorkshire pudding, Shepherd's pie, and Lancashire hot pot plus tea.

Baron Selsdon brought up an inquiry and said: "Elizabeth, how was your day? And how was the discussion to buy us out?"

Baroness was surprised and said annoyingly: "What offer? What are we selling?"

Baron Selsdon replied calmly: "We are trying to sell the company."

Baroness Selsdon continued with more anger: "Why would you sell our company without informing us all. You and your daughter should bring us into the decision making process!"

Baron Selsdon said peacefully: "My dear, relax. Elizabeth will fill us in. It is a windfall and it is meant to increase the wealth of the family! Let her speak."

Lady Selsdon started steadily: "Mom, do not be alarmed. We have this under control. Recently, our scientists developed a cure for diabetes which will raise the value of our Pharmaceutical Company from the current $1.2 billion to over $4.0 billion!"

Everyone was calmed, but full with attention and excitement.

Baroness Selsdon said probingly: "If this is true, then, why sell?"

Lady Selsdon continued: "We have not announced the news yet. It is good for us to sell because we could have close to $3.5 billion cash after tax to hold and invest in other businesses!"

Olivia jumped in and said enthusiastically: "That means that Jane and I will be very rich too and ripe for good suitors!"

Lady Selsdon ignored her comment and continued: "Astor Investment got an inside scoop of this finding and has made an offer to buy us 100% out for $4.5 billion. I rejected the offer!"

Baron Selsdon said curiously: "That is a good offer. Why reject it?"

Lady Selsdon continued and said: "I am not trying to play hardball, but I want to push them as high as we can get!"

Baron Selsdon said inquisitively: "What happens if they walk away from the table?"

Lady Selsdon said confidently: "No, they won't! They know that if the news gets out, then, there will be a lot of suitors rushing to buy us out!"

Baron Selsdon said happily: "Great job Elizabeth! Make it happen!"

Baroness Selsdon said worriedly: "Are you sure it is the right thing to do by selling off this company?"

Lady Selsdon said comfortingly: "Do not worry mother. I have this covered. Besides, I have a trick up my sleeves. When they come next time, I will tell them that we will keep 20% of the company plus the $4.5 billion offered!"

The dad busted out laughing and said: "Wow, child! You are a dangerous advocate! I feel sorry for the man that will marry you! Good Job Elizabeth!"

Everyone was smiling easily and was happy that Elizabeth was in charge of the negotiations.

Baron Selsdon said inquiringly: "When is the next meeting?"

Lady Selsdon said: "On the upper Tuesday. About 12 days from now. Three days after the Ascot Racecourse event."

Baroness Selsdon chipped in and said: "Good job Beth. The Ascot event is about nine days from today and we all have to go shopping for fine hats!"

Lady Selsdon responded and said: "Yes, mother. Let's go tomorrow with you and my sisters in the early morning. Then, I will meet with my friends in the afternoon for more hats' shopping since they will also be attending the events."

Baroness Selsdon continued: "Besides, your dad has two thoroughbred horses in the race and we will be routing for them to win!"

Lady Selsdon responded and said: "Ok, mother."

Baroness Selsdon saw an opening and asked shrewdly: "Also dear, it is time that you get married. I have some fine gentlemen that I will introduce to you at the Ascot Racecourse!"

Lady Selsdon responded belligerently: "Mother, I told you before to stop. I am capable of finding my own man!"

Baroness continued combatively: "I have not seen any new date with you. Your last date, eight months ago, you literally chased him away! You need a fine gentleman."

Baron Selsdon chipped in with a truce: "My dear, leave Elizabeth alone. Give her time to find the right man for her!"

They finished dinner and, Lady Selsdon and her sisters went upstairs to her room. They started kidding around and making jokes.

Olivia said: "Beth, for real, you are so beautiful that I cannot believe no man has asked you to marry him! You are getting older! You are too stubborn!"

Lady Selsdon said lovingly: "Olivia, I have had about eight men asking me to marry them. I refused because I do not love them!"

Jane joined the conversation and said: "But, sis, if you keep turning them down, then, you may be too old to find the right man! Why don't you find a handsome gentleman and learn to love him?"

Lady Selsdon said comfortingly: "Jane, that is a wonderful idea! If I do not find the man that I love in the next twelve months, then, I will do your bidding!"

The sisters agreed to the timeline and went to their quarters on the same 5th floor. Lady Selsdon closed her door and dialed her four friends by putting them on five-way conference call.

Lady Selsdon said to her friends: "Hey ladies! What have you wenches been doing?"

Lady Andrews, a blond-haired bombshell beauty from Scotland said scandalously: "Doing what you have not been doing! Fucking my man every day! Besides, you know sex is like playing bridge. If you don't have a good partner, then, you better have a good hand!"

They all fell out laughing frenziedly!

Lady Ashton, a brunette with wicked dimples and English beauty said wickedly: "Lady Andrews, that was crude! We don't care about you fucking schedule! Leave Lady

Selsdon out of it! She may not have a partner now, but I am sure she has very good and functional hands!"

The friends continued laughing uncontrollably!

Lady Adetutu, a black British beauty with parents from Nigeria and having a white teeth and one of the finest smile in London said supportively and mockingly: "I agree with Lady Ashton. Please leave Lady Selsdon out of your love live! In time she will find the pleasures in being in the hands of a fine gentleman!"

They all busted out laughing again.

Lady Bhatia, a British Beauty of Indian descent, with black beautiful hair and delicate fine features said shockingly: "My grandparents use to tell me that when a woman is at the age to be fucked by a man and she is not being touched, it will require huge pliers to open her up for sex!"

Everyone busted laughing and shaking with pains on their sides.

Lady Selsdon said matter-of-factly: "Ok, ladies. Enough of the smear! Get your minds out of the gutter! Fine gentlemen will be ashamed to hear you all talk!"

They all continued laughing.

Lady Andrews said outrageously: "Seriously, Lady Selsdon! Which planet are you from? The fine gentlemen talk dirtier than us and, quite frankly, love it when we talk sinfully like that!"

Lady Selsdon said: "I will find my own man soon and I will not need my hands anymore! Also, I will not have to come to you ladies with private parts as wide and deep as a well for extra coaching!"

They all started laughing frenziedly with tears in their eyes.

Lady Selsdon continued: "I called to remind you all to meet me tomorrow afternoon at about 1.30pm for hats' shopping for the Ascot Racecourse event. Meet me at Christys' and we will go from there to Bates, and, then, to Lock & Co. Hatters. We should be able to find some wicked hats between those three shops to 'wow' at the Ascot!"

The ladies all agreed to the date for Saturday and they said their 'good nights'. Lady Selsdon went to sleep around 11.00pm.

It was Saturday morning at 8.00am. The maid-in-waiting has already drawn Lady Selsdon's bath and woke her up to get ready for breakfast and for the shopping outing with her mom and sisters. She went downstairs and had breakfast with her family. Baroness Selsdon asked the butler to inform the chauffeur to bring the grey Bentley to the front.

Baroness Selsdon and her daughters got into the Bentley and were driven to the West End shops to shop for hats. Then, they went to Bond Street to a special hat store. The ladies tried various styles and colors.

Baroness Selsdon put on a yellow hat with peacock feathers. She asked: "How does this look?"

Olivia said: "You look dandy! Buy that one."

Jane added and said: "Yes, mom. You look swell in that hat!"

Jane chose a red wide hat and Olivia chose a green hat. Lady Selsdon chose a blue hat to match her blue eyes. They all modelled the hats and after that, they paid for the hats and left.

As they were heading home, Baroness Selsdon asked: "What are you all doing for lunch?"

Olivia said: "I am going to lunch with my boyfriend."

Jane said: "I am going to the movies with my boyfriend."

Lady Selsdon said: "Mother, do not wait for me. I am going further hat shopping with my friends and we are going to hang out in my apartment at Kensington Place."

Baroness said: "So, I will not be seeing you all for dinner?"

The sisters chorused and said: "No, mother!"

They got to their home and went to their various quarters to drop off their items. Lady Selsdon immediately went back downstairs and got in her red jaguar sports and drove to Christys' to meet up with her friends. She parked and went into the store. Her girlfriends were already there shopping.

Lady Selsdon said animatedly: "You all are already shopping without me!"

Lady Andrews said excitedly: "Yep. Just trying various styles and colors."

Lady Ashton said: "I like this wine one. What do you all think?"

Lady Adetutu said: "It looks cool on you. But, it is a spring-summer event. You need something vibrant!"

Lady Bhatia said: "Yes. I agree with Adetutu. Choose that orange color one instead."

The ladies did more shopping and bought bags and hats. They left Christys' and went to Bates and, finally ended at Lock & Co. Hatters. The ladies bought more bags and hats as they loaded their shopping items into their various cars. Then, they all drove to Lady Selsdon apartment at Kensington Place. They went upstairs and ordered dinner.

Lady Bhatia said breathlessly: "Next Saturday, at the Ascot, I am going to be looking fine and dandy, and hanging on the hand of my Prince charming!"

Lady Selsdon said inquiringly: "Who is that? Is he someone new?"

Lady Bhatia replied elatedly: "Yep. We were just introduced two weeks ago and I think I am in love with him!"

Lady Selsdon said excitedly: "Good for you! Maybe, I will be lucky and I will finally meet my Prince Charming next Saturday!"

Lady Bhatia said comfortingly: "Yep. I looked at my crystal ball and I saw a Prince Charming waiting for you next Saturday!"

They all busted out laughing.

Lady Adetutu said merrily: "Elizabeth, Lady Bhatia may be right. I saw it in my dreams too!"

They all laughed again.

Lady Adetutu continued and said seriously: "I am not kidding! It is going to happen! My dream always comes true!"

Lady Andrews said mockingly: "Adetutu, you had a dream for Elizabeth! How about your own dream for your Prince Charming? Did you see anything?"

They all busted out laughing hysterically.

Lady Adetutu said teasingly: "I will probably meet my Prince Charming there too! I will be looking so fine; he will be jumping the aisles to get to me!"

They all laughed uncontrollably again.

Lady Ashton said wickedly: "Andrews you better hold on to your man, because there are going to be some vipers present that will want to snatch him from you!"

Lady Andrews said jokingly: "I don't have to worry. I have his head so deep between my thighs that he is too engaged to see any lady!"

They all busted out laughing irrepressibly!

Lady Selsdon said: "Lady Ashton, are you coming with a date?"

Lady Ashton said morosely: "No. But, I will be putting myself out there and prancing so that I can be noticed as an art exhibition waiting to be bought!"

The ladies continued laughing wildly.

Lady Selsdon said teasingly: "It is not as bad as that. I believe the three of us left will find someone decent soon!"

Their dinner arrived and they started eating and drinking wine.

Lady Andrews said: "Ladies, I had a good time today. Let's do more of this the following Saturday after Ascot. But, for now, I am very horny and I am going to my lover's apartment to be fucked!"

Lady Ashton said sinfully: "Lady Andrews, stop behaving like a whore! Stay here with us till tomorrow!"

Lady Selsdon said wisely: "Yes, Lady Andrews, please stay. Besides you are too drunk to drive this evening!"

Lady Andrews said: "I am not drunk. Besides, you ladies do not understand. Seriously, I am very horny. I got to go!"

Lady Adetutu said jokingly: "You are giving too much toto to your man. You need to calm down until he put a ring on it!"

Lady Bhatia said inquiringly: "What is 'toto'?"

They all busted out laughing.

Lady Adetutu said wickedly: "That is colloquial or slang for your vagina!"

They all laughed again uncontrollably.

Lady Andrews said: "I understand. But, I got to go!"

They all bid her well and she left. The rest of the friends watched movies and stayed up late before going to bed in Lady Selsdon's apartment.

On Sunday morning at about 8.30am, they all got up and the friends went to their different homes. Lady Selsdon went back to her parents' home in Belgravia. She dressed hurriedly and accompanied her parents and sisters to church.

They got home from church at about 1.30pm and went and took light lunch. Then, they all retired to their quarters. Lady Selsdon decided to read a book for two hours before taking a nap for about two hours. She woke up at about 6.00pm and hurriedly took a bath as her maid-in-waiting came to announce that dinner was ready. She went downstairs to have dinner with her family and enjoy the rest of the evening.

Baroness Selsdon said inquiringly: "Elizabeth, will you be able to resolve the sale of our company this week?"

Lady Selsdon responded assuredly: "Yes, mother. It is possible. We will endeavor to conclude negotiations. It is not guaranteed that we will reach a conclusive agreement."

Baron Selsdon added: "Do you mean that we will be ready to sign an agreement this week?"

Lady Selsdon responded and said: "No, dad!! That is too quick. What I mean is that we may agree on a final figure and then draw up the initial draft agreement for your review and the board's approval."

Baron Selsdon said: "Ok. That sounds reasonable. Keep me updated on all negotiations."

Lady Selsdon responded and said: "Ok, dad."

Olivia said animatedly: "Lizzy, you mean in about two weeks I will be extremely rich!"

Lady Selsdon responded calmingly: "Olivia, you are already rich, anyway!!"

Baron Selsdon said in a controlling voice: "Olivia, you are already rich. But, you cannot touch that money!"

Olivia said annoyingly: "Why dad?"

Baron Selsdon responded firmly: "Because, I have placed your shares in trust and you will not be able to control it until you are forty years old. However, you will get monthly stipends enough to sustain your lifestyle."

Olivia said surprisingly: "Dad, that is not fair. If I was a son, you would have given it to me immediately. I know you did not do that for Lizzy!"

Baron Selsdon replied and said: "Olivia my dear, it does not matter if you were a male child or a female child. The trust framework will still be the same. It is put in place for your protection and to ensure that you are well-matured to understand the dangers inherent in having serious wealth and not knowing how to manage it. The same trust is in place for Elizabeth and Jane."

Baroness Selsdon addressed her husband and said: "Thank you my dear. I like the trust and I support your plan in ensuring that my girls are protected!"

Jane jumped into the conversion to reduce the tension and said: "Thank you dad for protecting us. I am interested in the Ascot Racecourse next Saturday. Can we discuss your plan in ensuring that your horses win next Saturday?"

Baron Selsdon said smilingly: "Jane, I do not know how we can enhance our chances since there are many fine horses in the race. However, our Jockeys are doing their best."

Lady Selsdon said: "Dad, mom, I am through with dinner. I am going to my room so that I can go to bed early. I have a lot to do in the office tomorrow."

Baroness Selsdon said: "Ok, Elizabeth. Sleep well and get plenty rest."

They all said their "Good nights" and went to their different apartments.

Chapter 3:

The Meeting at the Ascot Racecourse

It is 10am on Monday and Lady Selsdon is sitting in her office at Agar Pharmaceutical. There is great buzz and excitement going around the office as most workers have heard the rumors of the immense discovery at the company. They are discussing the possibility of receiving huge bonuses based on this scientific discovery. Her secretary informed her that all the executives were present at the boardroom. She got up and went to the boardroom. The executives got up as she came in, which was a respect for her position as a representative for her father, who is the chairman of the company.

Lady Selsdon said spiritedly: "Good morning everyone. Please sit down."

There were choruses of "Good morning" from the executives.

The Managing Director started and said excitedly: "Again, Good morning Lady Selsdon. Ladies and gentlemen, we are at an intersection of greatness for this company. The discovery has catapulted our company up as a major player in the global pharmaceutical industry. We all agreed to acquisition by Astor Investments for $4.5 billion. They are expecting us to agree in principle to this figure by this Thursday. A meeting is scheduled for this Thursday to sign the preliminary agreement. Of course, we all will be getting huge bonuses and keeping our jobs. We need to know where the family stands on this acquisition. Maybe Lady Selsdon can enlighten us."

Lady Selsdon responded and said firmly: "The family position is to sell. However, they have decided that they want to keep twenty percent of their stake in the company and maintain a minority holding in the company."

The Managing Director was worried and said: "Astor Investments may not agree to those terms."

Lady Selsdon said hopefully: "That is the family position. We shall present this position to them on Thursday and force them to accept our proposal."

After more discussions, the meeting came to an end. Lady Selsdon left and went to her office.

As she sat down, her phone rang. It was Lady Andrews and her friends.

Lady Andrews said lively: "Good morning Lady Selsdon. What are you up to?"

Lady Selsdon replied enthusiastically: "To what do I owe this pleasure of a surprise call from my fine ladies?"

Lady Andrews continued: "We want to give you a head up that we want to come to your place Thursday evening for a sleepover and discuss and model our dressing for the Ascot Racecourse on Saturday. And, then hang out the whole of Friday before going home. Is that OK by you?"

Lady Selsdon said inquiringly: "Do you mean that you do not want me to go to work on Friday?"

Lady Bhatia, Lady Adetutu, and Lady Ashton said together: "Yes! Please say yes my Lady!"

Lady Selsdon said excitedly: "Okay ladies! I will take off on Friday!"

The Ladies hollered on the phone excitedly as they say their "good byes".

At about the same, Lord Astor was being invited to the boardroom at Astor Investments. He got up from his chair and went to the boardroom. He wondered what the problem was that will necessitate an emergency meeting.

As he entered the boardroom, he saw that the executives were already seated.

They stood up and he said: "Good morning. Please sit down."

Lord Astor looked towards the Managing Director and continued: "Why are we having this meeting?"

The Managing Director said worriedly: "I just had a call from the Managing Director at Agar Pharmaceuticals and he told me that the acquisition could be in danger!"

Lord Astor said unhappily: "What do you mean? Do they want more money? I thought we already agreed on a final price?"

The Managing Director responded: "He did not tell me the actual issue. However, he said when we meet on Thursday he will inform us of a new modification to the agreement."

Lord Astor said: "If they are trying to play hardball, we will not buy into their modification. Let me know on Thursday, immediately after the meeting, what the modification is so that I can decide if we will move forward or not."

The Managing Director said: "The meeting is for 10am and I will call you immediately after the meeting."

Lord Astor said: "Good." And the meeting ended.

Lord Astor went back to his office feeling a bit troubled. At about 4.30pm, he left his office and went home. As he got in, he saw that his parents were in the study drinking brandy. Baron Astor noticed that something was wrong with his son.

Lord Astor said: "Good evening dad and mom."

Baroness Astor, unaware that his son was troubled, said: "Good evening son. How was your day?"

Lord Astor said: "Not too bad. Thank you mom."

Baron Astor said: "Lloyd, pour yourself a drink. Then, tell me what is ailing you!"

Lord Astor poured himself a brandy and said: "We have a problem with the acquisition of Agar Pharmaceuticals."

The Parents were both silent for a while.

Then, Baron Astor inquired and said: "What is the problem?"

Lord Astor said: "Agar Pharmaceutical wants to modify the purchase agreement. They may be trying to ask for more money which could render the deal unattractive."

Baroness Astor said encouragingly: "Maybe not. Maybe they just want to modify some terms in the agreement."

Baron Astor took a different stance and said: "Lloyd, do not despair. Let's find out what they want before deciding whether the deal will be attractive or unattractive. When will you know about the new request?"

Lord Astor replied and said: "Our team is meeting with them on Thursday."

Baron Astor responded and said: "Let's wait till then. In the meantime, go and change and come down for dinner. We are famished."

Lord Astor did as he was told and came back for dinner. After dinner he went to his room and called his girlfriend, Lady Chelsea.

Lady Chelsea picked up and said: "Hello my Lord. I was just about to call you!"

Lord Astor said cheekily: "My Lady, what is in your mind?"

Lady Chelsea replied elatedly: "The Ascot is on Saturday and I was wondering if you want me to come to your place on Thursday and we will go to the racecourse together."

Lord Astor said charmingly: "It sounds good, my Lady. Try and get to my place at about 7.00pm and we will have late dinner."

Lady Chelsea replied brazenly: "Ok, my special one. I will pack some night bags and bring all my costumes for the Ascot also.

Lord Astor said: "Great. See you on Thursday. Good night darling!"

Lord Chelsea replied salaciously and said: "Good night dear. I cannot wait to see you on Thursday!"

They hung up the phone. Lord Astor went to sleep.

It was Thursday morning at 10.00am at the Agar Pharmaceutical. In the boardroom, the executives of Agar Pharmaceutical and Astor Investments were already seated and waiting for Lady Selsdon. Ten minutes later, she came in and the executives stood up to welcome her to the boardroom.

Lady Selsdon said with a smile: "Good morning all of you. Please be seated."

All the executives sat down

Lady Selsdon, looking towards the Astor Investments' executives, continued and said: "The agreement to sell our company to you stands. However, we want $4.5

billion plus the retention of twenty percent in Agar Pharmaceuticals. That is our final offer. If you agree to this offer, then, we can draw the agreement and have both parties signed the documents in a meeting here next Thursday morning at 10.00am."

The Managing Director of Astor Investments responded: "Lady Selsdon, that is not what we agreed upon earlier. This modified offer will put a constrain on the sale. Our Principals will not agree to it."

Lady Selsdon replied firmly: "Tell your Principals that is our final offer."

Astor Investments' Managing Director said: "Please give me a minute and let me call my Principals."

Lady Selsdon nodded her head. The Managing Director got up and stepped out of the boardroom, and immediately place a call to Lord Astor. He narrated the new offer to him.

Lord Astor said: "Tell her we will do the deal if they agree to hold ten percent of the equity."

The Managing Director responded and said: "And if she refuses, then, what shall I tell her?"

Lord Astor replied and said: "Then, arrange a meeting for next Tuesday so that I can meet with her and discuss why our offer is best for her company."

The Managing Director said: "OK."

Then, he re-entered the boardroom and sat down.

He looked at Lady Selsdon and said: "My Principal made a counteroffer. He will accept the deal if your equity is ten percent."

Lady Selsdon said: "No. I told you before that our final offer involves the twenty percent in Agar Pharmaceuticals."

Astor Investments' Managing Director said: "My Principal will like a meeting with you next Tuesday Morning at 10.00am here in your office to conclude the agreement. Is this ok by you?"

Lady Selsdon replied: "Yes, that is fine by me."

She got up and brought the meeting to an end as everyone exchanged their pleasantries. Then, as they left, Astor Investments' Managing Director called Lord Astor and informed him of Lady Selsdon's insistence on twenty percent equity.

At about 4.00pm, Lord Astor left his office and went home. He narrated the event with the acquisition to his parents.

Baron Astor said: "What do you think? Should we walk away?'

Lord Astor said: "No, dad. We will not walk away. I will meet with her next Tuesday and try and convince her to accept the ten percent equity position."

Baroness Astor said daringly: "Make her accept it so that we can move forward."

Lord Astor said encouragingly: "Ok, mom. I will get it done."

Baroness Astor continued: "You have two hours before dinner is served."

Lord Astor said: "I will not be staying for dinner. I am going to my apartment in Knightsbridge since I have a dinner date with Lady Chelsea. I will stay there till I see you at the Ascot on Saturday."

Baron Astor said: "Ok. Get there early to our box so that we can plan winning strategies for our horses."

Lord Astor said: "Ok, dad. See you and mom on Saturday."

He left to pack his clothing and got in his navy-blue Aston Martin and drove to his apartment.

At about the same time on Thursday, Lady Selsdon got home and narrated the day's event to her parents.

Baron Selsdon said worriedly: "I hope they don't walk away!"

Lady Selsdon said assuredly: "They won't walk away."

Baroness Selsdon said: "Please accept the ten percent equity positioned offered so that they will not walk away from the deal."

Lady Selsdon said: "Ok, mom. I will conclude on Tuesday with them. Also, I am going to my apartment at Kensington Place now to meet with my girlfriends. They are sleeping over till Saturday. We will meet you at the Ascot on Saturday. They will be seating with us in our box."

Baroness Selsdon said warmly: "Ok, Elizabeth. You all should dress elegantly for Saturday."

Lady Selsdon said: "Ok, mom. Bye dad."

She left and went upstairs to pack her clothing and got back down as she got into her red Jaguar sports car. Then, she drove to her apartment in Kensington Place.

At about 6.30pm, Lady Selsdon's friends arrived at her five-bedroom apartment with all their clothing and hats. They all exchanged pleasantries and were each assigned a bedroom to sleep and hang up their clothing. Then, they all came to the living room and poured themselves various beverages.

Lady Selsdon said lively: "I am ravenous. What are we ordering for dinner?"

Lady Andrews said naughtily: "I do not know what you wenches are ordering. But, I will like to order an aphrodisiac prepped with boyfriend wheelie and have it stuffed down my throat!"

The Ladies laughed.

Lady Ashton said cheekily: "Lady Andrews, that is gross! We are not interested in that. Let's order food from that British restaurant next to the Chinese restaurant on the other side of Harrods. They will deliver."

Lady Adetutu said: "That is fine by me."

Lady Bhatia said: "That is fine by me too."

They all ordered various meals ranging from seafood to traditional British cuisine. When their meals arrived, they started eating, drinking and discussing their clothing for the Ascot. They stayed late into the night as they played music and danced. They went to bed at about 2.00am. They continued having fun throughout Friday. On Saturday morning, they got about 10.00am and dressed elegantly for the Ascot Racecourse event. Lady Selsdon requested that her dad should send the grey Bentley to take them to the Ascot.

Previously on Thursday at about 7.00am, Lady Chelsea knocked on Lord Astor's door at his Knightsbridge apartment. She came packing two bags with clothes and hats. Lord Astor helped her with her bags as she stepped up and kissed him. He took the bags and took them to the master bedroom and they came back to the living room as she was hanging on him.

Lord Astor inquired and said: "Are you ready to go out for dinner?"

Lady Chelsea replied sultrily: "No, darling. Let's eat in, then, I want you to fuck the hell out of me because I have been missing you since last weekend!"

Lord Astor laughed and said salaciously: "Much obliged, my Lady!"

And, then, He carried her up to the bedroom and laid her on the bed. He took of all her clothes as he ripped his own clothes off. She was lying naked in the bed looking up at him as he penetrated her. She started moaning and squirming loudly as they made love for over forty-five minutes. They both came to an orgasmic climax and lay side by side. He, then, got up and ordered dinner from an Italian restaurant for delivery. After dinner they made love again. On Friday, they made love throughout the day while stopping to eat breakfast and dinner.

At about 6.00pm on Friday, Lord Astor's friends called on a five-way call.

Lord Alton of Liverpool said eagerly: "Good evening Lord Astor. Are you getting ready for the Ascot tomorrow?'

Lord Astor said animatedly: "Good evening my Lords! Yes, I am getting ready. I want you guys to seat in my box with my parents."

Lord Anderson of Ipswich said gaily: "We will be there with our girlfriends!"

Lord Ahmad added enthusiastically: "We all are going to be dressed impeccably like serious British gentlemen!"

They all laughed. Lord Astor said: "Let's all do that!"

Lord Adeniyi added excitedly: "Also, do not forget that we all have a Polo match for the following Saturday!"

Lord Astor said: "It is noted. We all should plan to win the match!"

They all concluded and said their "Good byes".

On Saturday morning at about 10.00am, Lord Astor and Lady Chelsea got ready to go to the Ascot Racecourse. Lady Chelsea was wearing a fabulous and elegant green dress with a matching green hat. Lord Astor was dressed in a grey suit with a wicked gentleman's hat. They left his apartment and head to the Ascot.

The Royal Ascot Racecourse was first created in 1711 by Queen Anne who rode out of Windsor Castle and declared that the area was ideal for horse galloping. The race has continued every year since its opening and attracts over 300,000 racegoers during the five-day event. There are Lords, celebrities and wealth people from all over the world attending the event. Generally, the Queen and members of the Royal family are usually in attendance. There are about 225 private boxes at the racecourse which are generally owned by various Dukes, Viscounts, Earls, Barons, Lords, and wealthy British residences. There is a professional kitchen attached to every two boxes to provide fine dining for the box owners and their guests. The main private box belongs to the Queen. One of these 225 private boxes belongs to Baron Astor and another box belongs to Baron Selsdon.

At the Ascot Racecourse today, a lot of gentlemen and ladies are seen dressed impeccable and elegantly in various vibrant colors and heading to their various boxes and seats. Lord Astor and Lady Chelsea are seen heading to their box where they met with Baron Astor and Baroness Astor, who were fabulously dressed.

At about 12.00 noon, Lady Selsdon and her friends who were dressed fabulously, started moving elegantly towards their box to meet with her sisters and, Baron Selsdon and Baroness Selsdon. Lady Selsdon is dressed in an elegant blue dress and blue hat that matches her blue eyes.

Lord Astor is siting with Lady Chelsea and his friends close to Baron Astor and Baroness Astor. They are watching all the beautiful and elegant women coming to the stands, and some of them are accompanied by fine gentlemen that are flawlessly dressed.

Lord Alton said: "Lord Astor, when are you going to get us all beverages?"

Lord Astor replied: "Now. Who is coming with me to order?"

Lord Anderson said: "I will come."

Lord Ahmad said: "Please tell the servers to bring me Scotch whisky!"

Lord Adeniyi added and said: "Please tell them to bring me Bourbon!"

Lord Astor and Lord Anderson got up to head towards the private beverage stand and bar where box owners are specially served. At the same time, Lady Selsdon,

Lady Ashton and Lady Adetutu were heading towards the same private bar to order beverages for their box.

Lord Astor nearly collided with Lady Selsdon. He looked up and saw one of the most beautiful women he has ever laid his eyes on. His heart skipped a beat and was completely shaken and besotted by her beauty. Lady Selsdon looked up at Lord Astor and became suddenly weak in her legs. She had butterflies in her bellies and was smitten and captivated by him. He was one of the finest gentlemen she has ever seen. Her friends immediately saw the effect that Lord Astor had on her.

Lord Astor said spiritedly: "My Lady, pardon me for my clumsiness! I hope you are good!"

Lady Selsdon, tongue-tied, finally said: "My Lord, it is ok. I should have been watching where I was heading!"

Lord Astor said: "I am Lord Astor. My Lady, how should I address you?"

Lady Selsdon said: "I am Lady Selsdon. Nice to make your acquaintance!"

They shook hands, but Lord Astor refused to let go off her hands. She finally pulled her hands back to stop the fast beating of her heart.

Lord Astor will not let go. He continued: "Can I buy some drinks for you and your friends and I will have them sent to your box!"

Lady Selsdon said: "No my Lord. Do not bother."

Lord Astor said: "Please, my Lady. I insist."

Lady Selsdon did not want a conflict and to continue to argue with him. She said: "Ok. Our box is right there to my left." She pointed to were their box was.

Lord Astor said: "Thank you my Lady. I know that box. That is Baron Selsdon's box. He has some fine horses in the race. Your dad is Baron Selsdon?"

Lady Selsdon said: "Yes. Please bring us eight different drinks from Whisky, Bourbon to dry Gin. Just send the servers and we will tell them what else we need. Thank you."

Lord Astor said: "The pleasure is all mine, my Lady."

Lady Selsdon and her friends went back to their seats. She was still feeling shaken. She knows that she has finally found her 'Prince Charming'! Her friends knew something was up.

Lord Astor knew also that he has finally found the woman she has been looking for. He wondered if she was available. Regardless, he was determined to fight anyone to capture her heart.

He and his friends ordered and went back towards their seats. Lord Astor got up from his seat and went towards Baron Selsdon's box.

Lord Astor approached Baron Selsdon and said: "My Lord, good day to you and the Baroness. I wish you great luck in the race today for your horses."

Baron Selsdon said animatedly: "Thank you. Hope you are enjoying yourself. Wait. I know you. You are Lord Astor!"

Lord Astor responded: "Yes my Lord. And, I beg your indulgence to address your daughter."

Baroness Selsdon, instinctively thinking that this fine gentleman could be the right man, said excitedly: "Lord Astor, please feel free to address my daughter!"

Lord Astor said: "Thank you my Lady!"

Lord Astor, then, went towards Lady Selsdon and said: "My Lady, did the servers deliver your drinks?"

Lady Selsdon said breathlessly: "Yes, my Lord. Thank you!"

Lord Astor continued courageously: "Lady Selsdon, can I have your telephone number. Please?"

Lady Selsdon gave him her number and took his number.

Lord Astor said: "Thank you my Lady. I will call you so that we can do lunch next week. Is that ok?"

Lady Selsdon said: "Ok."

Lord Astor was very excited as he went back to his seat. Also, Lady Selsdon was expectantly happy for meeting with Lord Astor. Her friends knew something good was up. They started teasing her, but agreed to wait till later tonight to analyze what was just transpired.

In the meantime, at Lord Astor's box, Lady Chelsea saw what was happening and was trying to inquire from him what he was doing with the ladies in that box. However, Lord Astor told her that he was just visiting with friends. Lord Alton, Lord Anderson, Lord Ahmad, and Lord Adeniyi knew that a bombshell meeting just occurred and did not want to discuss what just ensued in front of Lady Chelsea. They intend to bring it up later on Sunday night when Lord Astor is not with Lady Chelsea.

The Ascot Racecourse was full with pomp and pageantry with the Queen in attendance. Baron Selsdon's horses did not win. The Ascot ended late in the afternoon as all guests are seen exiting the grounds.

Lady Selsdon and her friends went back to her apartment. Baron and Baroness Selsdon, and her daughters went home. Lord Astor and Lady Chelsea went back to his apartment, while his parents went back to their home in Belgravia.

Chapter 4:

One Grosvenor Square – Home of Baron Astor

It was early Saturday evening, about 7.00pm at Lord Astor's apartment in Knightsbridge. He and Lady Chelsea just came in from the Ascot Racecourse. Lady Chelsea was hanging over him as usual and kissing all up on him. However, Lord Astor's mind was preoccupied with the thoughts of Lady Selsdon. She has never seen a woman that beautiful with poise, elegance, gentle carriage, sophisticated and intelligence written all over her face. He was captivated and enchanted by her personality. Was this love or infatuation? He wondered.

Lady Chelsea sensed that something was amiss with Lord Astor. He was not responding to her touch as usual. She decided to dig further.

Lady Chelsea said worriedly: "My Lord, you seem troubled. You are not responding to my touch. Are you ok?"

Lord Astor lied and said tenderly: "I am okay, my dear. I was thinking about my meeting with my dad tomorrow."

She continued digging anxiously: "I saw you went to that box to speak to all the ladies in that box. Are you interested in any of them?"

He lied again and said: "My Lady, I am not interested in any of the ladies. The box belongs to Baron Selsdon and I went to say hello to him and wish him luck for his horses that are in the race. While there, it is respectful for me to wish his guests well!"

She said: "Do you know him before?"

He responded: "Yes. I have met him before through my dad."

She felt assured and change the topic, and said: "I am hungry. Are we going out or dinning in?"

He said: "Let me order some food for us so that we can dine in."

She said provocatively: "After food, can you fuck me the whole night? I am very horny!"

Lord Astor, still thinking about Lady Selsdon, responded and said: "Ok, my dear."

After the meal was delivered, Lord Astor served red wine with their food. As they finished eating, Lady Chelsea started playing with him. Lord Astor carried her to his bedroom and made forceful love to her for over one hour before they fell asleep.

They woke up late Sunday morning at about 11.00am. They made breakfast together and finished eat at about noon. They made love again before Lady Chelsea left for her own apartment. At about 2.30pm, Lord Astor left his apartment and drove to his parents' home at One Grosvenor Square.

At about 6.30pm on the same Saturday evening, after the Ascot Race, Lady Selsdon and her friends were dropped off at her apartment in Kensington Place in the grey Bentley. They got in and everyone started complaining that were hungry. They ordered their meals and changed into casual clothing. As they were eating, the fireworks started from Lady Selsdon's friends.

Lady Bhatia said jubilantly: "Ladies, I told you that I saw through my crystal ball that Lady Selsdon will find her Prince Charming today! I was right!"

Lady Adetutu said exultantly: "Ladies, I also told you that I had a dream that Lady Selsdon will find his Prince Charming today! I was right also!"

Lady Selsdon said mockingly: "Who will that be?"

Lady Adetutu said gleefully: "Of course, Lord Astor! He came asking for your phone number!"

Lady Andrews said jokingly: "Are you sure he is the Prince Charming? Or does he want to just fuck you! I saw a fine lady sitting with him. He is a playboy!"

Lady Selsdon perturbed, responded and said: "I hope he is not a playboy!"

Lady Ashton was there when they first met and was aware of Lord Astor's magnetic effect on her friend, and said seriously: "Elizabeth, do not listen to Lady

Andrews. From my observation, Lord Astor is smitten by you. Go for it. Play it right and capture his heart!"

Lady Selsdon responded worriedly: "You are right Ladies! For the first time, I think I am captivated by a man. And, I could be fallen in love with him. But, I am worried based on what Lady Andrews said that he could break my heart."

Lady Andrews, realizing the seriousness in Lady Selsdon's voice, stopped joking and said seriously: "I am sorry Elizabeth. I did not know you were enamored by him. Please let me know how I can help to capture him for you."

Lady Ashton said encouragingly: "Do not worry about his girlfriend. I did not see any ring on her fingers. We will all make sure he becomes your Prince Charming!"

Lady Adetutu said reassuringly also: "My Lady, do not worry. The stars are aligned in both of your stars. Lord Astor was so smitten by you that he left his date to come and ask for your number. Do not worry."

All the friends continued talking into the night before they fell asleep. They woke up early at about 7.30am and departed as they all plan to attend church with their families.

Lady Selsdon drove back to Mayfair to her parents' home so that she can get ready and drive with them to church.

As they were going to church, Olivia and Jane could not wait to ask Lady Selsdon about Lord Astor. But, Baroness Selsdon told them to hold their peace until they get home and after lunch. The Baron also told them to stay out of her business.

After church, the Baron Selsdon and his family sat down for lunch.

Olivia could not wait to start querying Lady Selsdon. She said: "Lizzy, that gentleman, Lord Astor is soft on you. Do you fancy him?"

Lady Selsdon responded demurely and said: "Yes, Olivia. I think he is a fine gentleman!"

Olivia and Jane giggled loudly.

Jane said animatedly: "Are you going to marry him? Is he your Prince Charming?"

Lady Selsdon said shyly: "I do not know. In affairs of the heart, there are two people involved. I do not know if he fancies me enough to want to marry me. Besides, that is too early to entertain."

Olivia pressed further and said: "If he asks you to marry him, will you accept?"

Lady Selsdon replied indignantly and said: "Olivia stop the bother. I saw him with a girlfriend. You know how men are. He is probably just checking me out. I do not know if he is serious."

Jane continued on the line of inquiry and said: "But, Beth, suppose he is crazy about you and abandon his girlfriend, will you accept to marry him?"

Lady Selsdon was getting annoyed and said: "Jane, let me be. I do not know."

Baroness Selsdon seeing that her daughter is disturbed and rattled by the inquiries realized that her daughter must be falling in love with Lord Astor. She must find a way to help her daughter.

She intervened and said warmly: "Olivia and Jane, please stop bothering your sister. Elizabeth, I see that for the first time that you are interested in Lord Astor. I will help you to ensure that the union between both of you becomes a reality!"

Lady Selsdon said genially: "Mom, thanks for your help. I am capable of determining my choice. Please step back and let me find my man."

Baron Selsdon tried to stay out of the discussion, but realizes that her daughter has been swept off her feet. He said: "I agree with Elizabeth. Please leave her alone. However, I know Lord Astor' parents and the young man is an eligible bachelor. Should you need my help, let me know."

Lady Selsdon said: "Thanks dads. I am fine."

They finished lunch and they all retired to their private quarters. Lady Selsdon was in love. She could not get Lord Astor from her mind. She wants to touch him and be held by him. She wondered if this is love or infatuation. Or, was she horny? She wishes he will call him!

At about 5.00pm and after anguishing thoughts, she decided to call her friends and narrate her dilemma in the hope that they will comfort her and give her solace. She placed a five way call to her friends.

Lady Selsdon said: "Hi ladies. I am in trouble!"

Lady Adetutu seems to figure out what the trouble was and said: "My lady, what is ailing you?"

Lady Selsdon said uncomfortably: "The affair of the heart ails me. I believe I am in love and I cannot get Lord Astor out of my mind. I am in trouble!"

Lady Bhatia said comfortingly: "Elizabeth, you are not in trouble. I think Lord Astor is probably thinking about you right now!"

Lady Andrews said saucily: "Sorry my Lady. Do not think too much of him. He is probably thinking about how to get between your legs!"

Lady Ashton said annoyingly: "Shut up Lady Andrews. Show some compassion. Lady Selsdon, do not listen to Lady Andrews. From what I saw, I think Lord Astor is probably crazy about you also!"

Lady Adetutu inquired and said: "Has he called you yet?"

Lady Selsdon said: "No. I am anxious. I wish he will call!"

Lady Bhatia said advisedly: "Do not be anxious. Be patient. Play hard to get. If not, he will get between your legs and leave!"

Lady Selsdon said weakly: "I want him to get between my legs. I am very horny for him!"

Lady Andrews busted out laughing! She said salaciously: "I know you have not been fucked well for a long time and you just can't wait to open your legs for him!"

All the other friends ignored her remark.

Lady Adetutu said nervously: "Wow Lady Selsdon. Calm down. Relax. Control yourself. There will be plenty of time for that. For now, play hardball. Please!"

Lady Selsdon said calmly: "I have heard you Lady Adetutu. I will control myself. I just wanted to share with you all on how I was feeling. There was fire all over my body as if I was burning. But, I will play hardball!"

Lady Bhatia responded happily and said: "Very good! Play hardball and all will be well!"

After more conversations, Lady Andrews, Lady Ashton, Lady Adetutu, and Lady Bhatia said 'good bye' to her and wished her well. Lady Selsdon rested awhile and then went downstairs for dinner at about 7.00pm.

On the same Sunday, at about 2.00pm, Lord Astor pulled up at One Grosvenor Square and immediately joined his parents for lunch.

Baron Astor said warmly: "How are you doing son?"

Lord Astor responded affectionately: "Good afternoon dad and mom. I am fine dad. Thanks."

Baroness Astor inquired: "Did you have fun at the Ascot?"

Lord Astor responded elatedly: "Yes, mom. I had a good time! I saw you and dad engaged with your friends and having a good time. I saw you and dad paying your respect to the Queen. You must have enjoyed yourselves!"

Baroness Astor said enthusiastically: "Yes, I did. Also, I saw that you and your friends were checking out the ladies and making passes as the ladies flirted around you all. You all had a jolly good time! Who is the lady that you went to talk to at Baron Selsdon's box?"

Lord Astor knew that his parents must have realized that he was enchanted by Lady Selsdon. He has not been able to get her out of his mind. She is extremely beautiful and poised with her deep blue eyes. He wants to hold her in his hands. He wants to make her his own forever. He wants to call her. He is feeling very anxious.

Lord Astor said lively: "Oh, yes! That is Lady Selsdon. Is she not beautiful?"

Baroness Astor realized that her son just confirmed her thoughts that he was enamored by Lady Selsdon! She said: "Are you interested in her?"

Lord Astor felt embarrassed that he could not hide his feelings and that his mom could read him so effortlessly! He said: "Yes, mother. Seriously, I think I may be falling in love with her. I know I just met her yesterday, but I cannot keep her from my mind! If she will accept me, I will marry her!"

Baron Astor jumped in and said pleasantly: "That is fast. You just met her. I hope it is not infatuation. What about Lady Chelsea?"

Lord Astor said charmingly: "It is not infatuation dad and mom. I know I am already falling in love with her. Besides, I told you earlier that I was not in love with Lady Chelsea. We are just having fun and dating!"

Baroness Astor said lovingly: "Ok, son. Go for her! I support your choice. But, are you sure she is not spoken for?"

Lord Astor said worriedly: "I don't think so. I did not see a ring in her hands."

Baroness Astor said: "Ok. Go for her and try not to break Lady Chelsea's heart."

Lord Astor said: "Ok mom. I will be gentle with Lady Chelsea if Lady Selsdon will have me!"

The all finished lunch and went to their different quarters. As Lord Astor finished undressing, he placed a five-way call to his friends.

Lord Astor said: "Hello guys! Hoped you all had fun yesterday at the Ascot!"

Lord Adeniyi said jokingly: "Yes, we had plenty fun. So many ladies to choose from! I found me a fine and gorgeous lady that went home with me!"

Lord Anderson said: "Yep, I had plenty fun with the horses and watching the bevy of beautiful ladies all around us. But, I could not do anything because my woman was watching me like a hawk!"

They all busted out laughing!

Lord Ahmad said: "Interesting Lord Anderson! My woman was watching me like an eagle ready to pounce on me if I turn my head towards any beauty! I had to watch from the side of my eyes!"

They all continued to laugh.

Lord Alton joined the conversation and said derisively: "I made a move on a very lady and I think she likes me! We will be having lunch next Wednesday!"

Lord Adeniyi said affably: "Lord Astor, I saw that you approached the lady in Baron Selsdon's box. She is one hell of a beauty! Who is she?"

Lord Astor said sprightly: "She is Lady Selsdon, daughter of Baron Selsdon. I am enamored with her! I am crazy about her! I am worried that she may already be spoken for and my heart will bleed if she will not have me!"

All the friends started laughing because they have never seen him so honest and defenseless for any lady.

Lord Ahmad said encouragingly: "Give her a call and see if she fancies you. If not, move on. You will not die and your heart will not bleed to death!"

The friends laughed again!

Lord Astor said: "I will give her a call this evening after dinner."

The friends conversed more and took leave of each other.

Lord Astor went downstairs to eat dinner with his parents at about 7.30pm.

As they were eating, Baron Astor said: "This new week is going to be very busy for you son. You have a meeting with the executives of Agar Pharmaceuticals on Tuesday and possibly closing of the deal by Thursday. Do you have a plan?"

Lord Astor responded and said: "Yes dad. Either way, we have to close the deal this week. If not competitors may get wind of the deal and that become problematic."

Baroness Astor seems interested in the love life of her son and said inquiringly: "Have you spoken to Lady Selsdon yet?"

Lord Astor replied sheepishly: "Not yet mother. I will try and talk to her after dinner. Hopefully, she will go out on a date with me!"

Baroness Astor said hearteningly: "I am sure she will! If she refused, give her a little time and then ask again. Keep asking until she say 'yes'!"

Lord Astor said blandly: "What happens if she never says 'yes'?"

Baroness Astor said reassuringly: "Then, move on. You will eventually find another beauty like her that will fall in love with you and that you will want to take to the altar!"

Lord Astor said: "Ok, mother. Thanks!"

They finished dinner and they retired to their separate quarters.

At about the same time, Lady Selsdon was having dinner with her sisters and parents.

Olivia started the conversion by bothering Lady Selsdon. She said worrisomely: "Has Lord Astor called you yet?"

Lady Selsdon responded indolently: "No. I will let you know when he calls!"

Jane said stridently: "Beth, you should call him. This is the 21st century and ladies are allowed to be aggressive!"

Lady Selsdon was rescued by her mother, Baroness Selsdon, who said correctively: "Ladies with good repute and fine upbringing don't do that! You should be ashamed of yourself, Jane! I know I taught you better than that!"

Jane said apologetically: "I am sorry mother. I know Beth is crazy about him and I just wanted her to reach out to him so that he will not slip away!"

Baroness Selsdon continued chidingly: "None of you should ever do that! Elizabeth, bid your time. Wait for him to call. That is Lady-like! I know you are enamored by him. But, you must play hard to get which makes you valuable to him! And, if he doesn't call, then, move on. You will eventually find the right man for you!"

Lady Selsdon responded gratefully and said: "Ok mother. I will do your bidding!"

Baron Selsdon jumped in to cool the atmosphere in the room by changing the subject. He said: "None of you empathized with me that my horses lost the race yesterday at the Ascot!"

Lady Selsdon said sympathetically: "Sorry dad. Maybe next time, your horses will do better!"

Olivia and Jane said in a chorus: "Sorry dad!"

Baron Selsdon said appreciatively: "Thank you all. Elizabeth, you have this deal this week that must be closed so that we can go on a much needed vacation!"

Lady Selsdon responded and said: "We will try and close the deal this week. A concluding meeting on Tuesday and a signing ceremony slated for Thursday. You have to be there on Thursday to sign as the Chairman of the company."

Baron Selsdon said: "I will definitely be there!"

They all finished dinner and went to their various apartments. At about 9.00pm, after Lady Selsdon has changed for bed, her phone rang. It was Lord Astor! Initially, she did not answer the call. The phone stopped ringing. She kept watching TV. Then, fifteen minutes later, he ranged again. This time, she picked up the phone.

Lord Astor said vibrantly: "Good evening my Lady. This is Lord Astor. I hope I am not disturbing your rest, and that I meet you at a good time?"

Lady Selsdon's heart was beating uncontrollably and she was having butterflies all over her tummy! She responded breathlessly: "Good evening my Lord. No, you are not disturbing me. How are you doing?"

Lord Astor's heart was also beating irrepressibly and grateful that she picked his call. When she heard her silky voice, he knew he was falling in love with her! He said: "I am doing well my lady. I am sorry your dad's horses lost yesterday. Please send him my regards."

Lady Selsdon found her voice and said: "Thank you Lord Astor. I will pass on the message."

Lord Astor did not know how to proceed without annoying Lady Selsdon, but decided to say what was in his mind courageously. He said awkwardly: "My Lady, please do not take offense to what I am about to say to you. And, I beg your indulgence to say it if you promise not to be annoyed with me!"

Lady Selsdon loves his voice and gentility, and was confirming in her mind that she was falling in love with Lord Astor! She said promisingly: "I will not hold it against you. Please say your mind."

Lord Astor said clumsily: "My Lady, since I met you yesterday, I have not been able to get you out of my mind! I am besotted with you! And, I want to know you more!"

Lady Selsdon was silent for a long time. What she heard was music to her ears. She nearly fainted with joy as her heart kept pounding.

Lord Astor was worried because of her nonresponse. He continued frightfully: "My Lady, I must have offended you! But you promised that you will not be offended!"

Lady Selsdon found her voice and said exultantly: "No, my Lord. You did not offend me! You caught me off balance!"

Lord Astor said hastily: "I am sorry my Lady. I did not mean to!"

Lady Selsdon continued relishing the moment and said: "It is alright Lord Astor. Are you enamored with me? Are you falling in love with me?"

Lord Astor said gratefully: "Yes, my Lady! I know I just met you yesterday. But, I believe I am falling for you. And, it is not infatuation!"

Lady Selsdon wanted to be sure that he was not just trying to get his way with her. She said: "My Lord, that is fast. Do you believe in love at first sight?"

Lord Astor said: "Normally, I will say that is a fable tale. But, since yesterday and throughout today, I have not been able to get you out of mind. Therefore, I believe that there is love at first sight!"

Lady Selsdon said: "Hmmmmm! Interesting my Lord."

Lord Astor was treading on a dangerous path and inquired worrisomely: "My Lady, did you not feel anything for me?"

Lady Selsdon lied and said: "Lord Astor, you are a fine gentleman. But, I have to know you more before I can decide if we share mutual feelings!"

Lord Astor cleverly saw an opening and said: "My Lady, can I buy you lunch tomorrow? And we can get a chance to know more about each other."

Lady Selsdon was secretively delighted about the request because she wanted to be close to him and feel him, and touch him! She replied and said; "Let's do lunch! Monday is not possible. Let's do Tuesday at noon!"

Lord Astor was excited and said: "Thank you my Lady! Should I pick you up?"

Lady Selsdon said: "No. I will text you a restaurant that we will meet. I will meet you there at noon on Tuesday."

Lord Astor said: "Thank you my Lady. I will see you on Tuesday. Good night!"

Lady Selsdon said: "Good night Lord Astor!"

They hung up the phone. Lord Astor was so excited that he wanted to call his friends and share the news. However, he decided to wait till Monday evening. Similarly, Lady Selsdon was exhilarated that she decided to call her friends and share the news also. But, it was late at night. So, she decided to wait till Monday evening.

Chapter 5:

Shopping Spree at Harrods

It was Monday evening at about 7.00pm and Lady Selsdon was having dinner with her family. She was excited and could not wait to share her news with her family.

As they sat down and began eating, Jane was anxious to hear if there was any new development in the love saga between her sister and Lord Astor. She inquired impatiently: "Good evening Beth. How was your day? Any news from your Prince Charming?"

Lady Selsdon partially ignored her and said: "Good evening Jane. I had a nice day. How was your day?"

Jane responded and said: "Good. You did not answer my question!"

Olivia jumped in curiously and said: "Hi Lizzy. Did he call?"

Baron Selsdon interjected and said: "Good evening my dear. How is the acquisition planning going?"

Lady Selsdon said: "Good evening Olivia. Good evening mom and dad. We are on schedule in our planning for the acquisition."

Baron Selsdon said: "Great! Let's enjoy our meal!"

Baroness Selsdon had intuition that something good was about to be shared by her daughter seeing that she has a pleasant demeanor. She said warmly: "Good evening Elizabeth. I see that you are please. You must have had a great day!"

Lady Selsdon said affectionately: "Yes, mother. I had a great day. Also, Lord Astor called me last night!"

Everyone was silent for a moment and expectant of great news.

Jane interrupted the quietness in the room and giggled. Then, Olivia joined her and both started giggling loudly.

Jane said elatedly: "I knew it! I sensed it! You were too happy when you came in!"

Olivia joined her and said: "I sensed it too! What did he say?"

Lady Selsdon said pleasantly: "He said he was enamored with me and that he is falling in love with me! I told him that I do not believe in love at first sight!"

Olivia and Jane started giggling excitedly.

Baroness Selsdon interrupted and said: "I believe in love at first sight! The very first day I met your dad, I knew I was in love with him!"

Baron Selsdon said: "Thank you my dear. Yes, your mother is right! I fell in love with her the very first day I laid my eyes on her! So, do not push him away. I do not think he is playing you."

Baroness Selsdon added: "I agree with your dad. Give him a chance."

Olivia inquired enthusiastically: "Are you in love with him?"

Lady Selsdon said breathlessly: "I will not push him away mother. I think I fancy him. I do not want my heart broken!"

Baroness Selsdon said encouragingly: "He will not break your heart. Give him a chance!"

Lady Selsdon quickly slides another news in and said: "We are having lunch together on Tuesday!"

Baroness Selsdon, happy that her daughter has finally found a gentleman that she is excited about, said hearteningly: "Go for it Elizabeth! Have fun! You may find out that both of you share mutual feelings for each other!"

Olivia and Jane supported their mother's view and encouraged her to have some fun.

Lady Selsdon said graciously: "Thank you mom and dad! Thank you Olivia and Jane! I will try and enjoy myself!"

They all finished dinner and retired to their private quarters.

As soon as Lady Selsdon got up to her bedroom, she picked up the phone and called her friends by putting them on a five-way conference call.

Lady Selsdon said animatedly: "Hi Ladies! How are you all doing?"

The friends could sense the excitement in her voice!

Lady Andrews said raunchily as usual: "Finally, my lady, you got laid after several months! You are so animated you are gushing over yourself!"

Everyone started laughing!

Lady Ashton said warmly: "Shut up Lady Andrews! Not every woman has a manhood permanently stuck between their legs like you! Please let the lady talk!"

They all busted out laughing!

Lady Adetutu joined the banter and said: "Seriously, lady Selsdon, did you make love today? You sound too happy!"

All the ladies started hollering with laughter!

Lady Selsdon said embarrassingly: "Far from it my ladies! But, my happiness stems from the fact that Lord Astor called me last night and professed his love for me!"

The ladies were quiet and taken back by the revelation!

Lady Bhatia said carefully: "Seriously! That is a red flag for me! I do not believe in love at first sight! I hope he is not trying to play you?"

Lady Ashton said reassuringly: "There is love at first sight! Do not listen to Lady Bhatia. There are several millions of first sight lovers that lived happily ever after!"

Lady Adetutu agreed and said: "I agree with Lady Ashton. Go for it my Lady!"

Lady Selsdon said gaily: "Thank you Lady Adetutu and Lady Ashton. I will go for it. I fancy him a lot! We are having lunch tomorrow. Let us all meet at Harrods on Wednesday or Thursday for lunch and shopping, and I will share with you how my date went."

They all agreed and said 'good nights'. Then, she sent a text to Lord Astor which read "meet me at The Clove

Club at 11.30am for early lunch". Lord Astor saw the message and replied back and texted back "Ok, my Lady! I will be there!"

At about the same time on Monday evening, about 9.00pm to be exact, Lord Astor was in his bedroom and decided to call his friends on a five-way conference call and share the news with them.

Lord Astor said: "Good evening fine gentlemen!"

The friends chorused "Good evening Lord Astor!" The friends noticed that he was very excited.

Lord Adeniyi said jokingly: "What excites you my Lord?"

Lord Astor continued jubilantly: "I got a date!"

Lord Alton said inquiringly: "What are you talking about?"

Lord Astor said happily: "I told you all that I am falling in love with Lady Selsdon. Well, I told her last night and I am having a lunch date with her tomorrow!"

Lord Anderson said quixotically: "You mean you told her you love her after just meeting her within twenty-fours!

Do you know how unrealistic that may sound to her? She will think that you are trying to play her!"

Lord Astor said: "I know I should not have said that. But it is the truth. I am falling in love with her and I hope she does not see me as a player. Hopefully, she will allow me to prove it!"

Lord Ahmad said reassuringly: "Go for it my Lord! What are you going to do with Lady Chelsea?"

Lord Astor responded bewilderedly: "I do not know. If Lady Selsdon accepts my love, then, I will have to find a gentler and kinder way to break my relationship with Lady Chelsea."

The friends wished him good luck and reminded him of their Polo match for next Saturday. Lord Astor went to sleep elated.

It is 9.00am at the headquarters of Astor Investments, Lord Astor and his top executives are planning to head towards Agar Pharmaceuticals. They left at about 9.30am.

They got to Agar Pharmaceuticals headquarters at about 9.55am. They were ushered into the boardroom where

Agar Pharmaceuticals' executives where already seated. They exchanged greetings and Lord Astor was asked to seat at the end of the table as they wait for the arrival of Lady Selsdon.

She came in about 10.02am and said: "Good morning gentlemen!" Then, she sat down.

She was unaware that Lord Astor was in the room. She said: "Can we start?"

Lord Astor saw her and his heart started racing like a schoolboy! He did not know and it did not register in his mind that Lady Selsdon was the person in charge of Agar Pharmaceuticals! Wow! He was blown away!

The Managing Director of Astor Investments rose up and introduced everyone in his team including Lord Astor. Then, Lady Selsdon noticed Lord Astor and blushed with her heart beating uncontrollably!

After a moment, she composed herself and said: "My Lord, my apologies. I did not know you are here and that you the head of Astor Investments. It did not connect. I am sorry!"

Lord Astor said embarrassingly: "My Lady, my sincere apologies too. I was not aware that you are in charge of Agar Pharmaceuticals. If you want, I will step out and let our executives finalize the deal!"

Lady Selsdon said: "Lord Astor, it will be your choice!"

Lord Astor said: "I will leave. My apologies!"

He got up and wished all well as he exited the boardroom.

Lord Astor drove around and finally got to The Clove Club at 11.20am. He waited at the bar for ten minutes and, then, Lady Selsdon came in at about 11.30am.

Lord Astor got up from the bar and hugged Lady Selsdon. Then, they were directed to a private table in the rear of the restaurant. They sat down and ordered their meals.

Lord Astor said apologetically: "My Lady, I apologize for this morning. Sincerely, I did not know that you were in charge of the company."

Lady Selsdon said equally regretful: "My Lord, it is mutual. I did not know that you were in charge of Astor Investments."

Lord Astor said warmly: "To confirm that I did not know that you were in charge of Agar Pharmaceuticals, I will not demand that you drop your request for twenty percent of the equity!"

Lady Selsdon said also warmly: "Lord Astor, thank you! In order for you to know that I accept your apology and, also to confirm that I was not aware that you were in charge of Astor Investments, I will accept your offer that we keep ten percent of the equity and not twenty percent that I was requesting earlier!"

Lord Astor said elatedly: "My Lady, thank you. You just made my day! You are kind and compassionate! And, I am scarred that I am falling in love with you!"

Lady Selsdon was overjoyed too and said: "My Lord, why should you be scarred to fall in love with me?"

Lord Astor said worriedly: "Because I do not want you to break my heart since I do not know your feelings for me now!"

Lady Selsdon responded lovingly and said: "Of course my Lord, I do have some feelings for you! If not, I will not be having lunch with you!"

Lord Astor tried to push the envelope further and said: "But, does it rise to the level of love?"

Lady Selsdon responded receptively and said: "I just met you, my Lord. I have to know you more. Your values, your integrity, your moral standing, and your empathy! Are you a kind soul? Are you a decent human being? What are your likes and dislikes? And other elements that form the human framework. But, it all starts with a feeling which then transforms to love as we spend time together. The feelings for you are there already! Let's see if it transforms to love!"

Lord Astor said wisely: "That is fair my Lady. Then, we should spend more time together! Right?"

Lady Selsdon said agreeingly: "Right. Let's do more of that!"

Lord Astor was happy and saw more openings. He said: "My Lady, should we then try and see one another at least four times a week? A mixture of lunch and dinner?"

Lady Selsdon said agreeably: "That sounds fair! I suggest Monday, Wednesday, Friday and Saturday."

Lord Astor said tenderly: "That is a deal! I promise I will be at my best behavior and natural. Hopefully, you will fall in love with me!"

Lady Selsdon laughed and was having a good time. She said: "Let's see. But, please be natural!"

Lord Astor was enjoying himself also and said: "I will be natural. Can we see tomorrow for lunch and, Friday and Saturday for Dinner?"

Lady Selsdon said: "Tomorrow is out. I have a lunch date with my girlfriends at Harrods. Let's do dinner for Thursday, Friday and Saturday."

Lord Astor was pleased and said: "That sounds good to me. Also, my Lady, I am having a Polo match on Saturday morning and I want you to accompany me. Is that okay by you?"

Lady Selsdon said tenderly: "Ok, Lord Astor. Also, do not forget that you and your executives will be at our office on Thursday morning at 10.00am to sign the final agreement for the acquisition."

Lord Astor said: "Thank you my Lady. We will be there."

They finished their lunch at about 1.30pm and stood up to exit the restaurant. Lord Astor walked Lady Selsdon to her car and kissed her on the full lips before she entered her car. She kissed him back and got in her car and drove back to her office. She was so happy that she has finally found her Prince Charming! She knew that she is in love with him, but tried to hide that fact from him. She got to her office and announced to her executives that the acquisition deal has been agreed upon and will be signed on Thursday morning. Everyone in the company was happy because they will receive huge bonuses and their jobs are guaranteed.

Lord Astor was exhilarated and on ecstatic meltdown. He was in love and knows that Lady Selsdon have feelings for him. He drove to his office and announced to his own executives that the acquisition deal has been agreed upon and will be signed on Thursday morning. All members of staff of the company were happy because they will receive huge bonuses.

After getting home and changing, and at about 7.00pm on the same Tuesday, Lady Selsdon went down to have dinner with her family. She was feeling very jubilant and has plenty of news to share with her family. Everyone noticed the change in her demeanor and the glow on her face.

Lady Selsdon said: "Good evening mom and dad! Olivia and Jane, good evening!"

Everyone said good evening.

Baron Selsdon said inquiringly: "Elizabeth, we are anxious. How were your meetings today?"

Olivia chirped in and said: "And, also, what happened at your lunch date?"

Lady Selsdon said enthusiastically: "We have a deal! The acquisition will be signed on Thursday and dad you have to be there. We agreed on keeping ten percent of the equity!"

They all clapped, laughed and congratulated Lady Selsdon for a job well done.

Jane said exultantly: "I am rich! Thank you Beth! Now, about your date?"

Lady Selsdon said elatedly: "My date with Lord Astor was wonderful! Had a good time! He professed his love for me! I assessed he is real! And, I am beginning to have strong feelings for him!"

Olivia jumped and clapped and giggled loudly. She said: "Yes! I am finally going to attend a wedding of my big sister!"

Baroness Selsdon said calmly: "Sit down Olivia. We are happy for Elizabeth. But, give them time to develop their love for each other. Great news Elizabeth!"

They finished dinner and all retired to their private quarters.

Likewise, after returning from the office and changing, and at about 7.30pm, Lord Astor went downstairs to have dinner with his parents. His face was radiant with happiness.

Lord Astor said animatedly: "Good evening mom and dad!"

Baron Astor said: "Good evening son. Sit down and let's eat. And, then tell us about your escapades today!"

Baroness Astor added lovingly: "And, especially your lunch date!"

Lord Astor said: "Dad and mom, we have a deal! You are seeing the new billionaire on the block! Agar

Pharmaceuticals agreed to keep ten percent equity and we will be signing the new deal on Thursday morning! Dad, you have to be there."

The parents were happy and congratulated their son for a good job!

Baron Astor said: "Great job son!"

Lord Astor continued: "And I had a great lunch date! I believe Lady Selsdon share the same feelings I have for her! In fact, she is virtually the main decision maker on the deal and I did not know earlier. She, actually, ensured that the deal was agreed upon!"

Baroness Astor said expectantly: "Does that mean I see marriage on the horizon?"

Lord Astor said: "Hopefully, mother! I will like to very much marry her! But, I need to work on it and get her to the same place I am now!"

Baroness Astor is excited and happy that his son has finally found a woman that he loves and considering for marriage. She said: "I will be praying for you son. She will be the one!"

Lord Astor said: "Thank you mother!"

They finished their meals and went to their private quarters.

Lord Astor called his friends on a five-way conference line and informed them of the good news with regards to his lunch date with Lady Selsdon.

Lord Astor said excitedly: "Good evening my friends! I had a great lunch date! And, I have found the one that I have been seeking!"

Lord Alton said: "Great my friend! I am happy for you!"

Lord Astor said: "Thank you Lord Alton!"

Lord Anderson said inquisitively: "Does that mean that you intend to marry her?"

Lord Astor responded and said: "I sure will if she will have me!"

Lord Ahmad said: "When will you propose to her?"

Lord Astor responded energetically: "Very soon, I hope! I will give you all a head start before I propose!"

Lord Adeniyi said receptively: "Very good, my friend! When can we meet her?"

Lord Astor said: "On Saturday at the Polo match. She will be my guest and I will introduce her to you guys."

The friends were happy for Lord Astor and they all said their 'Good nights'.

At about 9.30pm on the same Tuesday evening, Lord Astor decided to call Lady Selsdon. She picked up his call.

Lord Astor said amorously: "Good evening, my love! Thank you for lunch today."

Lady Selsdon was delighted and said tenderly: "Good evening my Lord. I enjoyed myself. Thank you very much."

Lord Astor said: "You are welcome my Lady!"

They spoked more for about thirty minutes before they bid each other 'Good night'.

It was Wednesday afternoon at about 1.30pm and Lady Selsdon walked into Harrods to meet with her friends. They ate lunch in one of the restaurants in Harrods before deciding on shopping. While eating, Lady Selsdon decided to narrate the events of her lunch date with Lord Astor.

Lady Selsdon said joyously: "Ladies, I think I am falling in love!"

Lady Bhatia said interestingly: "Who will that be?"

Lady Selsdon replied and said elatedly: "Lord Astor of course! We had a great lunch date yesterday and I enjoyed our meeting! He told me that he was in love with me!"

Lady Adetutu said tenderly: "I am happy for you my Lady! Does that mean that you will marry him if he proposes?"

Lady Selsdon said exuberantly: "Yes, I will marry him. I am falling in love with him!"

Lady Andrews asked good-humoredly: "You are falling in love with a man you just met under a week? My lady, are you crazy? Besides, she has a girlfriend. Did you ask him about his girlfriend?"

Lady Selsdon said a bit disconcerted: "I have not asked about that yet. But, I will be asking about her this week and requesting that he tells me about his intention for her and for me too!"

Lady Ashton said amiably: "Elizabeth, do not be worried. If he prefers her girlfriend, he would have proposed to her. I strongly believe that he is in love with you! Relax and enjoy the Lord, my Lady!"

Lady Selsdon said gaily: "Thank you Lady Ashton. I will enjoy it and see if he really loves me! By the way, he kissed me yesterday!"

Lady Andrews said: "Oh no! His intentions are sleazy and sinful. He just wants to get into your pants quickly and run away!"

Lady Selsdon said defensively: "I do not think that are his intentions. Nonetheless, If that is his sole intention, then I welcome it! I will like to get laid by him!"

All the friends started hollering and laughing!

Lady Andrews said mockingly: "I knew it! You are now Lady Whore! You have not been fucked for several months and all you want to do is open your legs wide and be royally fucked by Lord Astor!"

They all busted out laughing and hollering!

Lady Selsdon said animatedly: "You are right! I want to be royally fucked by Lord Astor!"

They all started laughing and hollering out loud so much that people in the restaurant were looking at them!

Lady Andrews continued scornfully: "I knew you had it in you! What a dirty language from a prim and proper English Lady!"

Lady Selsdon said sardonically: "An English Lady loves fucking too! There is nothing wrong with the usage of my language even for a prim and proper English Lady, my dear Lady Andrews!"

The friends all busted out laughing irrepressibly and hollering again!

Lady Ashton said supportively: "Lady Selsdon, please go ahead and fuck your English gentleman!"

There were more laughter and hollering!

Lady Selsdon said: "In addition, besides fucking him, I intend to marry him!"

The friends continued laughing uncontrollably and clapping their hands!

They finished their lunch and went shopping inside Harrods. They left with lots of bags of clothing items. Lady Selsdon went home and had dinner with her family as they prepared for Thursday signing of the agreement.

At about 9.30pm, Lord Astor called her. They spoke for about forty-five minutes. He professes his love again for her. They hung up and went to sleep.

Chapter 6:

At Ham Polo Club, Richmond

It was Thursday morning at 10.00am and the executives of Agar Pharmaceuticals and Astor Investments were in the boardroom reading over the agreement. On one side of the table were Baron Selsdon, Lady Selsdon and their executives. On the other side of the table were Baron Astor, Lord Astor, and their executives.

As they finished, Lord Astor stood up and said favorably: "Again, good morning my Lady, Lords and all executives. Today is a historic day for both of our companies. Agar Pharmaceuticals will get all the funding and support it needs to move to the next level in its industry. And, Astor Investments will continue to be an Investment Banker of repute. This agreement solidifies our relationships. Thank you."

He sat down as everyone applauded.

Lady Selsdon stood up and said happily: "My Lords, and all our executives, I share the sentiments of Lord Astor on this historic moment. Where is the champagne? This has to be popped to celebrate this occasion!"

A giant bottle of champagne was rolled in and popped. Then, everyone was served as they all stood up to toast the occasion.

Lady Selsdon continued and said: "I toast to everyone!" Everyone toasted and sipped their drinks.

She continued: "I applaud all our executives and everyone that worked hard to make this deal a reality! Thank you everyone!"

They all applauded as she sat down.

Baron Astor stood up and gave a laudatory message and said: "Baron Selsdon, Lady Selsdon, Lord Astor and all our executives, I laud all your efforts and cooperation. Thank you. Let's sign this document and continue celebrating!"

There were a lot of applauses and smiling from everyone.

Baron Selsdon also stood up and gave a congratulatory message and said: "My good friend, Baron Astor, I did not foresee this recent event happening! The new drug discovery brought us together and will solidify our relationships. My gratitude to Lady Selsdon, Lord Astor and all our executives for the terrific good job you all did! I agree with my friend. Let's sign this document! Cheers to everyone!"

They all applauded as the agreement was signed!

They finished and they all started to exit the boardroom.

As they were leaving, Lord Astor pulled Lady Selsdon aside and said: "For our date this evening, should I pick you up?"

Lady Selsdon asked curiously: "What restaurant are we going to?"

He replied and said: "The French House around Mayfair. Is that ok?"

She answered and said: "It is ok. Yes, you can pick me up at my apartment in Kensington Place at 6.30pm, Hold up. Let me send you my address now."

She immediately sends him a text with her address.

He saw the text and said: "I got it. I will see you at 6.30pm!"

They said their 'Good byes'. The executives and the staff of Agar Pharmaceuticals came and congratulated Baron Selsdon and Lady Selsdon as they entered their private offices.

Lady Selsdon got home at 4.30pm and joined her family as they celebrate the successful acquisition. She told them that she will not be joining them for dinner since she has a dinner date with Lord Astor. She left thirty minutes later with a night bag full with different clothing items and drove her red Jaguar sports car to her apartment at Kensington Place. She took a shower and put on a lilac dress with a Christian Dior black Jacket, and a black pump. She looked smashingly beautiful!

She examined herself in the mirror and smiled. She knew she was wickedly beautiful! She said to herself: "Eat your hearts out, Lord Astor!"

At One Grosvenor Square, Lord Astor informed his parents that he was having dinner with Lady Selsdon and may stay late. He wore a stripped and light brown jacket on a black pant, and was looking extremely debonair. He got in his blue Aston Martin and drove towards Lady Selsdon's apartment.

At exactly 6.30pm, He buzzed the doorbell at Lady Selsdon's apartment. Lady Selsdon opened the door and Lord Astor's heart skipped several beats. He looked and examined Lady Selsdon and concluded that she was an exquisitely beautiful woman! An exotic and gorgeous beauty! Likewise, when Lady Selsdon saw Lord Astor, she became weak in the legs as she examines the devilishly handsome gentleman with a wicked smile. She knew she was in trouble!

Lord Astor said with a tremor in his voice: "My Lady, you are divinely beautiful!"

Lady Selsdon smiled and said: "Thank you my Lord. You look extremely suave yourself!"

Lord Astor walked her to the car and opened the door for her. They drove towards the restaurant as they discussed the acquisition events that took place today. They got to the restaurant and were ushered to their seats by the hostess. They sat down and ordered their meals plus a bottle of champagne as they continued to celebrate the acquisition deal. Lord Astor ordered a steak dinner while Lady Selsdon ordered a French cuisine lamb. Their meals arrived and they started eating.

Lord Astor said warmly: "My love, you know with you heading Agar Investments, I will be seeing more of you every day!"

Lady Selsdon smiled and said: "Seriously! Are you moving your office next to mine?"

He laughed and said: "No my Lady! I meant colloquially!"

She laughed and said: "My dear Lord Astor, why don't you say exactly what you mean?"

He continued laughing and said: "I mean, I will like to see you every day!"

She continued laughing and said: "Better! How do you intend to accomplish this feat or endeavor?"

He busted out laughing. He was enjoying her company and completely enamored by her. He said: "By you moving into my apartment permanently!"

She giggled out loudly and said: "My dear Lord Astor, I just told you that you should say what you mean! What exactly do you mean?"

He laughed more and said: "I mean I want you to be mine! I want you in my life permanently! And can you please call me Lloyd?"

She was quiet for a moment as she ponders his response. She said: "Are you proposing to me Lloyd? I barely know you!"

She laughed more.

He responded and said: "My love, it is a preliminary proposal which I intend to make very formal later! I love you my Lady!"

His response was sweet music to her ears. She was excited that Lord Astor meant what he was saying!

She said tenderly: "Lloyd, I must confess that I am beginning to be very fond of you. And I seem to be falling in love with you!"

This was one of the best news that Lord Astor has heard in his lifetime! He was suddenly quiet and taken aback!

He jumped up and went to Lady Selsdon side and lifted her up and kissed her fully in the mouth! She kissed him back! He put her down and went back to his seat.

He said: "Thank you my love! Your intelligence and beauty bedazzles me!"

Lady Selsdon giggled and said: "You are welcome, my dear!"

Lord Astor said stupidly: "Will you be coming to my apartment tonight?"

Lady Selsdon said indignantly: "Absolutely not, my Lord!"

He quickly said apologetically: "I did not mean it like that my love! In my gratefulness of your professing your love for me, I was anxious to be close to you. I am sorry, my Lady. Take your time and let me know whenever you are ready to spend private time with me!"

She said amorously: "Ok, Lloyd. I forgive you. Besides, whatever happened to your girlfriend I saw you with at the Ascot?"

He responded contritely: "That is Lady Chelsea. She is a good person, but, I do not love her! I am madly in love with you! Regretfully, I will have to tell her so that she can move on with her life. I have never professed my love to her like I did you. Hopefully, she will not be too hurt and will move on with her life."

She said sincerely: "I am glad you are compassionate!"

He responded and said: "I sent you a text earlier while we are eating. Please read it."

She took her phone and read the text which said: "Lady Selsdon, I really love you. If you will have me, I will seriously like to marry you."

She smiled, but with tears in her eyes.

He said contritely: "I am sorry dear. I did not mean to hurt you!"

She responded with a smile: "I am not hurt. It is tears of joy! I do not know whether I like the new technology of texting! I still like the old art of writing. Can you put it in writing to me?"

Lord Astor was exhilarated and said: "I definitely will have it for you tomorrow when we have dinner!"

She sent him a text immediately which said: "Lord Astor, I will have you and gladly marry you."

He received the text and was deliriously ecstatic. He got up again and went to her side and kissed her deeply and said: "Thank you my love!"

They talked more and left the restaurant about 9.00pm. He drove her to her apartment and, then went home.

Lady Selsdon got into her red Jaguar sports car and drove back to her parents' home in Belgravia. She was too excited. She got in and saw that her parents and her sisters were still in the study watching television and playing backgammon.

Lady Selsdon said animatedly: "Good evening mom and dad. Good evening Olivia and Jane."

They all responded and said 'Good evening Elizabeth'.

Lady Selsdon shouted jubilantly: "Lord Astor proposed to me that he wants to marry me!"

They all shouted and hollered, and laughed as they celebrated with her.

Lady Selsdon got close to them and showed the text that Lord Astor sent her. She said: "He will make the proposal formal later!"

Baroness Selsdon said lovingly: "Elizabeth, it finally happened! I am happy for you my dear!"

Lady Selsdon said happily: "Thank you mother!"

Olivia said joyously: "Lizzy, I am glad for you!

Lady Selsdon said: "Thank you Olivia!"

Jane said: "Beth, congratulations! I am pleased that I will finally be able to plan a wedding with mother for my big sister!"

Lady Selsdon said: "Thank you Jane!"

Baron Selsdon said joyously: "My daughter, I am so happy for you!"

After more conversations, everyone retired to their private quarters.

As Lady Selsdon got to her bedroom and changed, her friends called.

Lady Selsdon said exuberantly: "Good evening Ladies. He proposed!"

They all hollered and laughed on the phone!

Lady Andrews said obscenely: "Tell the truth my Lady. You allowed him to fuck you today after dinner!"

Lady Selsdon said seriously: "No, Lady Andrews. He did not fuck me! You are a guttersnipe! Get your mind out of the gutters!"

They all busted out laughing!

Lady Selsdon continued and said: "In fact, he told me I do not have to sleep with him until I am ready and till we are married!"

Lady Ashton made a congratulatory statement and said: "My Lady, congratulations! The only way Lady Andrews can ever get married is to open her legs for every gentleman in Belgravia!"

All the Ladies busted out laughing again!

Lady Adetutu and said encouragingly: "I am pleased with you my lady. I told you last week that I dreamed that that you will find your Prince Charming at the Ascot! It Happened!"

Lady Selsdon said gaily: "Yes, you did, my Lady! Thank you. I really appreciate you, Lady Adetutu!"

Lady Bhatia joined in and said: "Congratulations my Lady! Also, remember I told you that I saw in my crystal ball that you will find your Prince Charming at the Ascot! And, it happened!"

Lady Selsdon said: "Thank you, Lady Bhatia. I will be having Dinner with him tomorrow night and watch him play Polo on Saturday morning."

Lady Selsdon continued: "I want you all to come to the Polo match with me on Saturday morning and meet with him and support his team. I will text you the address tomorrow and time."

The friends agreed to attend and they all said 'Good nights'.

At about the same time, that Thursday, Lord Astor called his friends.

Lord Astor said merrily: "Good evening friends. I have great news for you guys!"

Lord Adeniyi said curiously: "Good evening Lloyd. What's up?"

Lord Astor announced exuberantly: "Gentlemen, I asked Lady Selsdon to marry me this evening at dinner and she accepted!"

The friends were silent for a while. Then, they started clapping and bawling.

Lord Anderson said happily: "I am happy for you my friend. That is fast though. You just met her a week ago!"

Lord Astor said: "True, it is fast. But, I love her and she professed her love for me. So, we are good!"

Lord Ahmad inquired and said: "So, we should be ready to celebrate a wedding soon?"

Lord Astor responded and said: "Yes, a wedding will be celebrated soon. However, I only asked her to marry me. I intend to make a formal proposal within a week! Then, the plans for the wedding will start in earnest!"

Lord Alton said: "Congratulations my Lord. Let us know what we need to do to make this happen!"

Lord Astor said: "Thank you Lord Alton. Let's start by you meeting her on Saturday morning. She will come and watch us play the Polo match. Also, I will tell her to bring her friends if she wants to."

They all finished conversing and said 'Good nights' to each other.

At 9.30pm, Lady Chelsea called Lord Astor. Lord Astor knew he has a tough job ahead: how to break up with Lady Chelsea amicably! He picked up the phone.

Lord Astor said jovially: "Good evening my dear."

Lady Chelsea said amorously: "Good evening my darling! How was your day?"

Lord Astor said: "My day was good. Thank you my Lady. How was yours?"

Lady Chelsea said seductively: "My day was ok. But, I am missing you terribly! I need your shagging! I am coming to your place early tomorrow evening. I want you to fuck me as I entered your apartment and all night!"

Lord Astor knew, sadly, that he will not be sleeping with Lady Chelsea ever again. It was the end of the road for both of them.

Lord Astor lied and said disappointedly: "Sorry my Lady, we will not be seeing this weekend. I have to accompany my dad to an important event this weekend. But, I will come to your apartment on Tuesday evening by 5.00pm!"

Lady Chelsea was shell-shocked and disappointed. She said: "Oh, no! What am I going to do with myself this weekend?"

Lord Astor said upliftingly: "Do not worry. We will see on Tuesday."

After small talks, they said good night and hung up the phone.

At about 10.00pm, Lord Astor called Lady Selsdon to wish her good night. He told her that he will pick her up tomorrow at her apartment at 6.30pm for dinner.

It was Friday and Lady Selsdon got home at about 4.30pm to prepare to get some clothing items and drive to her apartment and be picked up by Lord Astor. She decided to wear Tiffany-colored green dress and wine-colored jacket with wine-colored pumps. She looked delicately beautiful and elegant.

Lord Astor was well dressed in an impeccable navy blue jacket and black pants with black shoe. He was looking suave. He walked to Lady Selsdon's door and pressed the buzzer. She opened the door and was looking alluringly beautiful. Lord Astor was tongue-tied!

Lord Astor said hypnotically: "My love, your beauty is spellbinding! Let's go."

Lady Selsdon said seductively: "Thank you my dear! You look intoxicatingly handsome yourself! What restaurant are we going?"

Lord Astor responded and said: "Let's try St John restaurant around Knightsbridge."

Lady Selsdon said: "Ok."

They got into his navy-blue Aston Martin and drove to the restaurant. The host knows Lord Astor and took them to a special private room. They ordered their meals. Both of them decided to have seafood dinner that comprises of cod and vegetables plus a bottle of white wine.

As they were eating, Lord Astor took out an envelope from his inside jacket and gave it to her.

She said curiously: "What is it?"

He said lovingly: "You requested I put it in writing. I did. I love you so much that I want to marry you! Read it later tonight."

Lady Selsdon smiled and said: "Thank you, my love! That is sweet. I will cherish it forever!"

He smiled and said: "Thank you darling!"

Lady Selsdon said pleasantly: 'For tomorrow morning, can I invite my girlfriends to the game?"

He responded and said: "Yes of course! And, you will get to meet my friends, also! It is at the Ham Polo Club in Richmond."

She said: "Ok."

Then, she texted the address to her friends and told them to be there at 10.00am.

Lord Astor said lovingly: "My Lady, after the game, will you come to my apartment before we go out for dinner?"

She said tenderly: "Ok, my dear!"

They finished their meals and he drove her back to her apartment. He kissed her passionately and left as he drove back to his own apartment.

On Saturday morning at about 9.00am, Lord Astor dressed in polo outfit and drove to the Ham Polo Club. He got there at about 9.45am. At about the same time, his friends, Lord Alton, Lord Anderson, Lord Ahmad, and Lord Adeniyi drove up too.

Lord Alton said cheerfully: "Good morning Lord Astor. Are you ready to kick their asses today?"

Lord Astor said jovially: "Let's strategize and see how we can beat them!"

Lord Anderson said: "We can do it. Let's go to the dressing rooms and get ready."

Lord Ahmad asked inquisitively: "Where is your betrothed? We will like to meet with her before the match starts!"

Lord Adeniyi joined in the conversation and said: "Yes, Lord Astor, where is your fiancée?"

As Lord Astor was about to answer, he saw five cars drove in. He saw Lady Selsdon in the red Jaguar sport car and her four friends driving behind her.

Lord Astor said: "Here she is now!"

Lady Selsdon stepped out of the car wearing white pants and black blouse with riding boots. She was looking smashingly beautiful! Her friends stepped out too and walked alongside her as they approached Lord Astor and his friends.

Lord Astor went towards Lady Selsdon and kissed her. He said: "Good morning my Love! Please introduce me to your friends. Then, I will introduce you to my friends."

Lady Selsdon responded lovingly and said: "Good morning darling. Meet my friends, Lady Andrews, Lady Ashton, Lady Adetutu, and Lady Bhatia!"

Lord Astor said cordially: "Nice meeting you Ladies! Please enjoy the match."

Lady Andrews said: "Wow, you are a handsome devil. You must treat my friend lovingly!"

Lady Ashton said: "Nice to meet you Lord Astor."

Lady Adetutu said: "Lord Astor, my friend is a very good lady. Treat her well or I will break your legs!"

Lady Bhatia said: "Nice meeting you Lord Astor!"

Lord Astor said: "Thank you my Ladies for your great compliments. I will treat my beloved fiancée with love and care!"

Lord Astor, then, took the hands of Lady Selsdon and walked with her towards his friends.

He said: "My love, please meet my friends, Lord Alton, Lord Anderson, Lord Ahmad, and Lord Adeniyi."

Lady Selsdon shook their hands and said: "It is a pleasure meeting with you all, my Lords."

Lord Alton said: "My Lady, you are extremely beautiful! Nice to meet with you!"

Lord Anderson said: "My Lady, you are simply gorgeous! I see why my friend is crazy about you!"

Lord Ahmad said: "My Lady, it is a pleasure to meet with you! Let me know if I can be of any help!"

Lord Adeniyi said: "It is nice meeting you Lady Selsdon. I can't wait to be at your wedding!"

Lady Selsdon said: "Thank you my Lords. I appreciate all your kind gestures to me."

Lord Astor told his friends that they should go to the dressing rooms and get ready for the game. While, the Ladies went to the stands to watch the Polo match. Lord Astor's team won the match.

After the match, everyone went their separate ways, except for Lord Astor and Lady Selsdon. Both of them drove to his apartment at Knightsbridge.

Chapter 7:

Back at One Grosvenor Square

It was Saturday afternoon at about 4.00pm, and Lord Astor and Lady Selsdon just walked into his apartment. He went close to Lady Selsdon and started kissing her passionately.

Lady Selsdon pulled back and said affectionately: "My darling, you are sweaty! Go have a bath!"

He answered teasingly: "Yes, my Lady. I will do that!"

She said approvingly: "Your apartment is furnished tastefully and fabulously! I like the colors chosen. Who was your designer?"

He responded diplomatically: "An Italian designer on Bond Street. I cannot recollect his name. Thank you for appreciating my taste!"

He said: "Give me a moment to freshen up."

He went into the bedroom to use the master bathroom and take a shower. Lady Selsdon went to the expansive living room and sat down while looking at his book and music collections. About thirty minutes later, Lord Astor came back wearing casual slack and top, and joined Lady Selsdon in the living room. He sat close to her and held her hands.

She asked curiously: "How many bedrooms do you have in your Townhouse?"

He answered and said: "Five bedrooms. Plenty of space for everyone!"

She ignored the connotation in his statement and said: "Why I asked is because your Townhouse is similar to mine and I have five bedrooms too!"

He said nicely: "Great! I am starving. Are we eating in or going out for dinner?"

She responded pleasantly: "Let's eat in. If we go out, I will have to go to my apartment and get dressed up. I don't feel like that!"

He responded and said: "Ok. What type of cuisine are you interested in for dinner Lady Selsdon?"

She said affectionately: "Lloyd, please call me Elizabeth. And, can we try authentic English cuisine today?"

Lord Astor answered and said lovingly: "Ok, Elizabeth! I will address you as my heart feels!"

She answered and said tenderly: "Ok, darling!"

He got up and said: "Let me go ahead and order now. It takes them about forty-five minutes to deliver here. We should be eating by 6.00pm."

After a moment, he came back and said: "I saw you were looking at my music collections. Should I play some music and pour you some drink?"

She responded and said: "Yes. Play some Beatles. I was looking at your book collections also. At least, it reveals that you are learned and appreciate reading!"

He laughed and played the requested music. Then, he said lively: "Ok. You mean that you would have rejected my advances if I was an illiterate? Seriously?"

She laughed and said earnestly: "Of course I would have rejected you! Because you will not have the capacity to engage in intelligent discussions! Besides, you will not be too creative in all affairs, including our bedroom!"

He busted out laughing in frenzy!

He responded and said: "My love, I can debate the merits of your conclusions all day and I will come out on top! Firstly, your assertion that illiterate men cannot be creative in bed is utterly fallacious!"

She started laughing too and said: "My Lord, my assertion is based on scientific fact! Can you support your position?"

Lord Astor was loving the moment and enjoying her company: "I do not have to support it with facts. It is intuitional. It is everywhere. Our illiterate ancestors were very creative in their bedrooms. Their wives did not have to complain. I can bet you they were better in bed than our current literate gigolos!"

She continued laughing and said: "My dearest gentleman, you cannot win this argument! Let's defer the defense of our positions for other times. And, please be ready to debate other issues as it arises with factual materials throughout our lovely and endearing relationship, and as husband and wife!"

He said: "Aha, you stand down. You know Elizabeth, I seriously love you! Should I pour you something to drink?"

She said amorously: "I love you too, Lloyd! Please pour me Scotch Whiskey."

He poured two glasses and gave her one. As he sat down close to her, she pulled an envelope from her bag and gave it to him.

He inquired curiously: "What is this?"

She responded with a smile and giggles and said: "My response to your love letter you gave me yesterday. I read your letter and I loved it! I hope you love my response!"

He was about to open the envelope when she said: "No. Do not open it now. Open it after I am gone!"

He put the letter on the side table and said: "Ok, I will do that. I thought you will spend the night here with me today?"

She smiled disarmingly: "Not tonight, my love. Some other time. We have plenty of time to spend the night together! Besides, I have to go to church tomorrow with my family."

He responded and said beguilingly: "Ok, my Lady."

Then, he got close to her and started kissing her passionately. She kissed him back and feeling very wet. She could feel his erection pressing on her pants. Then, she stopped and pulled away.

She said tenderly: "Not now my love! I am not ready! You told me to take my time. I will let you know when I am ready!"

He said understandingly: "Ok, darling. There is no rush. We have all our lives to enjoy each other."

He continued jokingly: "You can have all the time till our honeymoon! Then, our bed will be rocking!"

She laughed out loudly: "My Lord, I am not that old fashion! Chastity is good, but I will not keep you burning for that long, darling!"

He laughed out loud and said: "Elizabeth, you are something else! For you I will burn!"

She laughed loudly and ecstatically!

At that time, their food arrived and they started eating. At about 7.00pm, Lord Astor walked Lady Selsdon to her car and watched her drive off heading to her parents' home.

As Lord Astor sat down to watch tv, his friends called and put him on a five-way conference call.

Lord Astor said animatedly: "Good evening fine English Gentlemen!"

Lord Adeniyi said excitedly: "Good evening, Lord Astor. Your fiancée is an extremely beautiful woman! You are lucky to find her. I am surprised she has evaded the fine gentlemen in London. Keep her well! I have a request: I will like to meet Lady Adetutu. She is extremely beautiful too!"

Lord Astor responded sparklingly: "Thank you my Lord! I will endeavor to keep her! Also, I will ask Lady Selsdon if Lady Adetutu is available!"

Lord Ahmad added enthusiastically: "Lord Astor, your fiancée is extremely gorgeous! You need to put a ring on her finger quickly before another fine gentleman takes her way from you!"

Lord Astor said elatedly: "Lord Ahmad, I am happy that you approve of her. I am meeting with a jeweler next week to design a fine ring for her. I intend to formally propose to her by next weekend or thereabout!"

Lord Alton added to the conversation enthusiastically: "Lady Selsdon is an exotic beauty! I agree with Lord Ahmad that you have to quickly put a ring on her finger before you lose her. Have you set a wedding date in your mind?"

Lord Astor replied genially: "Thanks Lord Alton. I will discuss with Lady Selsdon and see if we can put our wedding on a calendar for under sixty days from now. You all should get ready for the biggest wedding in London!"

Lord Anderson said amiably: "I am happy for you my friend. You are a fine Gentleman and a great catch. I am sure Lady Selsdon is happy and fortunate to have captured your heart!"

Lord Astor said: "Thank you Lord Anderson. I will try and be a good husband to her!"

They had more conversations before they hung up. Lord Astor decided to sleep at his apartment tonight and head back to his parents' home, tomorrow, Sunday.

At about the same time, around 8.00pm, Saturday evening, Lady Selsdon came downstairs and joined her family in the drawing room.

Lady Selsdon said lovingly: "Good evening mom and dad. Olivia and Jane, nice evening to both of you!"

Baron Selsdon said fondly: "Good evening Elizabeth. How was the Polo match?"

Lady Selsdon responded and said merrily: "I enjoyed it thoroughly! Lord Astor's team won. I had a great time!"

Baron Selsdon continued: "Do you know when the funds from the sale will be transferred to our account? So that I can move the funds to the various investment accounts."

Lady Selsdon said reassuringly: "It should be in our account before next Friday!"

Baron Selsdon said gratefully: "Thank you Elizabeth for a fine job!"

Baroness Selsdon joined the conversation and said inquiringly: "How is your relationship with Lord Astor going on?"

Lady Selsdon said elatedly: "It is going well mother. I will be having lunch and dinner dates with him next week for Monday, Wednesday, Friday, and Saturday."

Olivia said happily: "Thank you Lizzy, for making me a very rich woman! What date have you chosen for your wedding?"

Lady Selsdon said charmingly: "Olivia, that is not proper etiquette! There has to be a formal proposal and engagement before a date for the wedding is chosen. I will let you know when we get to that point!"

Jane said stridently: "Beth, when is the proposal and when shall we know the wedding date? I want to go shopping for beautiful clothes for your wedding!"

Lady Selsdon said happily: "Lord Astor has made a formal proposal by asking me to marry him through his letter he wrote to me. I have accepted his proposal by writing a letter to him which I delivered to him today!"

Lady Selsdon pulled out the letter in his bag from Lord Astor and started reading it to them. Then, she read her own acceptance letter to him. They were all happy for her as they await the formal engagement. She bid them good night and went to her own quarters.

As she got to her room and finished changing for bed, her friends called on a five-way conference line.

Lady Selsdon said exuberantly: "Good evening my lovely Ladies! What ails your hearts this evening?"

They all started laughing!

Lady Andrews said mockingly: "What ails my heart is how the heck did you steal such a fine and handsome gentleman from me! I should be the one having Lord Astor and not you!"

All the ladies started laughing uncontrollably!

Lady Selsdon responded winningly: "Lady Andrews, no way in hell will I let you get close to my man with your dirty mind!"

The ladies started hollering and laughing!

Lady Ashton said excitedly: "Elizabeth, Lord Astor is a handsome hunk of a man! Wow! I did not know he was so devilishly good-looking! You need to quickly get him to put a ring on your fingers before someone else try to snatch him! And, please keep him away from Lady Anderson!"

The Ladies kept laughing uncontrollably!

Lady Selsdon responded belligerently: "Thank you Lady Ashton! I am working on it to ensure I get the ring on my fingers quickly and keep English whores like Lady Anderson away from him!"

They all laughed irrepressibly again as they were shouting on the phone!

Lady Adetutu said warmly: "Good evening Elizabeth! Yes, your future husband is a very attractive, gorgeous and striking gentleman. Please get engaged quickly so that we can help you plan a wedding!"

Lady Selsdon said appreciatively: "Thank you, Lady Adetutu! You know you are my loving angel! I am working towards that goal!"

Lady Bhatia joined in the banter and said enthusiastically: "Elizabeth, your wedding is here! Let's start preparing! We need to go to the Mayfair Gallery of Bridal Group, Inc. and look at wedding gowns and gowns for bridesmaid. What do you all think?"

Lady Selsdon said gaily: "That is a fantastic idea, Lady Bhatia! Can we all do lunch next Thursday at about 1.00pm and, then, stop at the gallery to see what they have for bridal wears?"

The friends all agreed to meet on Thursday and they hung up the phone. Lady Selsdon went to bed late as she was thinking about Lord Astor.

It was Sunday afternoon at One Grosvenor Square. Lord Astor was about to have lunch with his parents.

Lord Astor said elatedly: "Good afternoon mom and dad!"

Baron Astor responded affectionately: "Good afternoon son. How was your Polo match?"

Lord Astor said winningly: "It went well. We played hard and we won well. Lady Selsdon was there with her friends to watch us play."

Baroness Astor added warmly: "I am glad that you and Lady Selsdon are spending quality times together! She is a heck of a beauty. Do not tarry so that she does not slip away from your hands!"

Lord Astor said assuredly: "I will not let her slip away from me, mother. I love her a lot! I have formally proposed to her in a letter I gave to her on Friday. And, she has accepted my proposal via a letter she gave to me yesterday! I intend to announce our engagement within two weeks and set a wedding date for six weeks from now. I will officially try and meet with her parents to ask for hands in marriage within the next week and bring her to meet with you and dad!"

Baroness Astor was elated that his son has finally found a lady she is in love with and ready to marry. She said happily: "Thank you Lloyd! I am very happy for you!"

Lord Astor replied thankfully: "Thank you mother!"

Baron Astor inquired interestedly: "Son, has our bank wired the funds for the acquisition to the two companies' accounts involved?"

Lord Astor responded and said: "They have notified us that the funds will be wired next Thursday."

Baron Astor said: "Great! That is concluded and you are a very rich man!"

Lord Astor said: Thank you dad!"

After Lunch, they all retired to their separate quarters.

Lord Astor went to his bedroom and read, and, then, took a nap. When he got up at about 6.00pm, he thought about calling Lady Selsdon. Then, he decided against it and chose to wait till after dinner. After dinner, Lord Astor called Lady Selsdon. She picked up the phone.

Lord Astor said lovingly: "Good evening sweetheart! How is my Lady faring?"

Lady Selsdon said seductively: "Good evening my love! Your Lady is faring well!"

He said cravingly: "I missed you the whole day! I wished you were here by my side!"

She said provocatively: "My heart ails for you my love! I have been thinking about you the whole day too! And, I wish I was there in your hands!"

He continued and said brazenly: "Why don't you put on your clothes and I will come and get you now!"

She said comfortingly: "No my love! Be patient with me!"

He said amenably: "Ok my dear. Are we doing lunch or dinner tomorrow?"

She said enchantingly: "Of course my love! I cannot wait to see you! Besides, I want you to kiss me! Let's do lunch instead. Then, let's do lunch for Wednesday, and dinner for Friday and Saturday!"

Lord Astor was happy that she cannot wait to see him and said delightfully: "Ok, my love. We shall do as you suggested."

She continued lovingly: "I will be dreaming about you tonight!"

He said steamily: "I hope it will be indecent love-making!"

She laughed seductively and said: "I hope so! Besides, there is nothing indecent between two betrothed lovers!"

Lord Astor said lovingly: "Very true my Lady! I read your acceptance letter and it was the sweetest letter I have ever read! Thank you my darling!"

Lady Selsdon said approvingly: "You flatter me my Lord! My letter is simple and from the heart! I bet you have read plenty of finer letters!"

He responded earnestly: "My Lady, I am not flattering you. I mean what I said. It is best I have ever read. Simply the best! Thank you for accepting to be my wife! I will endeavor to make you very happy!"

She said tenderly: "Thank you my Lord. I promise to make you very happy too!"

He said amorously: "Thank you darling! I know you will make happy!"

She inquired pleasantly: "Where are we meeting for lunch tomorrow, and what time?'

Lord Astor responded gratifyingly: "Let's meet at Six Portland Road restaurant at 1.30pm. They have good steaks!"

She said agreeably: "That sounds good! I feel like eating steak too!"

They said 'Good night' to each other and went to bed.

It was Monday morning at about 11.00am, Lord Astor left his office and went to the famous jeweler in Belgravia. He was shown several pieces of diamonds and he chose two to be crafted for Lady Selsdon. The first set comprises of an engagement ring with a pear-shaped four carat diamond which was of the highest quality and sparkle. He paid $250,000 for it. He told the jewelers he will pick that up on Wednesday morning at 12.00 noon. The second set comprises of three rings: the engagement ring and two wedding bands. The engagement ring was set on a platinum band with seven-carat diamond of the highest quality and sparkle. The two wedding bands were each crafted with simultaneous stones of sapphire and diamonds to match Lady Selsdon's eyes. He used his little index finger to determine the size of Lady Selsdon's ring finger. He paid $750,000 for this set.

At about 1.00pm, Lord Astor left the jewelers and head for his lunch date with Lady Selsdon. He got to the restaurant at about 1.25pm and waited in the lobby for Lady Selsdon. At exactly 1.30pm, Lady Selsdon walked into the restaurant. She was looking radiantly beautiful. She walked with a poise and elegance that captivates the sinful fantasy of most men. She is a dangerous beauty! Lord Astor wondered why no other gentleman has swept her off her feet! He considered himself extremely lucky to have captured her heart!

He got up and got close to her, and kissed her passionately in the mouth claiming what now belongs to him. She kissed him back fervently as some of the diners looked on with envy!

Then, they pulled apart as the hostess took them to a private section of the restaurant. They both ordered steak meals plus red wine.

Lord Astor said satisfyingly: "Sorry my love! I was missing you and I could not help myself!"

Lady Selsdon said lusciously: "Do not be sorry darling! I wanted you to kiss me passionately and you obliged me as if you were reading my mind! I loved it!"

Lord Astor said: "Thank you sweetie!"

Their meals were served and they started eating.

Lord Astor said inquiringly: "I will like to meet with your parents and formally request your hand in marriage from them so that they can approve of our union! What time this week will be appropriate?"

Lady Selsdon was astounded and happy. She said lovingly: "Why don't you come to my parents' house in Mayfair at

7.00pm on Thursday and have dinner with us. I will inform them that you are coming."

He responded graciously and said: "That is fine by me. And, I want you to come to my parents' house at One Grosvenor Square for dinner at 7.00pm on Saturday. I will let them know that you are coming. Is this good?"

She responded happily: "Yes, darling! It is good. Also, I just sent you a text with my parents' address."

He said: "I got it."

She inquired amusingly: "Where are we doing lunch on Wednesday seeing that you are spoiling me and trying to fatten me for the kill!"

He laughed out loud and said wittingly: "My lady, my intention is innocent! If you are not fattened, then, the kill will literarily break you into small pieces!"

She laughed out loudly and said seductively: "My Lord, are you saying that my frame is not strong enough to withstand your pounding?"

He continued laughing and said enjoyably: "Far from it my Lady! You are very pliable! However, you need fattening to ensure that there is enough flesh to be served after the killing!"

Lady Selsdon said wickedly: "My fine gentleman, you have a sinful and mischievous thought! Wow! What will I do with you?"

Lord Astor, still laughing and having a good time, said wantonly: "Do to me my Lady what you want me to do to you!"

Lady Selsdon was having an extremely good time and said alluringly: "My Lord, you have wicked wits and if you do to me what I want to do to you, we will have monumental problem!"

Lord Astor busted out laughing as most diners turned their way to see them enjoying themselves. He said devotedly: "My Elizabeth, I love you so much!"

She responded and said dotingly: "I love you a bunch, my Lloyd!"

He said: "For Wednesday, let's do lunch at 1.30pm at the Black Axe Mangal. It is a fine restaurant close to Mayfair."

She said: "Ok. Will see you there, darling!"

They finished lunch and went back to their offices. At about 4.30pm, Lady Selsdon went home to her parents' house. Similarly, at about 5.00pm, Lord Astor left his office and went home to his parents' home at One Grosvenor Square.

Chapter 8:

Mayfair Gallery of Bridal Group, Inc., London

At about 7.00pm, the same Monday, Lady Selsdon went downstairs to have dinner with her family.

Lady Selsdon said warmly: "Good evening mom and dad. Olivia and Jane, fine evening to both of you!"

Baron Selsdon said tenderly: "Good evening Elizabeth! Sit down and let's eat this sumptuous dinner!"

Baroness Selsdon continued lovingly: "Good evening dear!"

Olivia said affectionately: "Good evening my special sister!"

Lady Selsdon said tenderly: "Thank you Olivia. That is very sweet of you!"

Jane said jealously: "Olivia, I thought I was your favorite sister! I am annoyed with you!"

Olivia said: "Jane, you must be dense in the head! You do not know the difference between special and favorite!"

Jane, trying to get back at Olivia, said teasingly: "Good evening Beth. You are my special and favorite sister!"

Lady Selsdon said kindheartedly: "Thank you Jane!"

They all continued eating.

Then, Lady Selsdon said excitedly: "Mom and Dad, I have invited Lord Astor to dine with us on Thursday evening. Is that ok by both of you?"

Baron Selsdon said affectionately: "Of course, my dear! He is welcome. I look forward to meeting with him!"

Baroness Selsdon has an inkling of what this means. She said eagerly: "Yes, my dear. He is welcome!"

Olivia joined in the conversation and said enthusiastically: "I get to meet your Prince Charming. I bet he is very handsome!"

Jane, not wanting to be left out of the conversation, said breathlessly: "Great! I will be officially meeting my future brother-in law!"

Lady Selsdon, addressing her mother and father, said happily: "He wants to meet with both of you so that he can officially ask your approval for my hand in marriage!"

Everyone hollered, laughed, and clapped in pure joy for Lady Selsdon. In what the family was never used to: they saw, suddenly, the usually reserved Baroness Selsdon got up and started dancing around the table. Then, Olivia and Jane got up and joined their mother and started dancing around the table also as they sang 'ring around the roses'. Even, the usual reticent Baron Selsdon, joined in the merriment!

Baron Selsdon continued laughing and said enthusiastically: "I approve!"

Baroness Selsdon said happily: "I approve also! I was worried for you Elizabeth. I thought it will be hard for you marry because you have very high expectation and standard in the man you wanted! I am glad that you have found love at last!"

Lady Selsdon said gaily: "Thank you mother! Correction, though. It is not that my standards and expectations were high, but, I needed to find a man that I was in love with!"

As if her approval was needed, Olivia said vivaciously: "You have my approval too!"

Jane said effervescently: "I wholeheartedly approve!"

They all finished their dinner and retired merrily to their individual quarters.

At about 6.45pm, on the same Monday, Lord Astor went downstairs to have dinner with his family.

Lord Astor said spiritedly: "Good evening mom and dad. I hoped you had a brilliant day!"

Baron Astor said warmly: "Good evening, son. Yes, my day was great! How was yours"

Lord Astor said: "Splendid! I had a wonderful day!"

Baroness Astor said sprightly: "Great! I see that you are happy! My day was very good!"

Baron Astor said lovingly: "Sit down and let's have dinner."

They sat down and started eating.

Then, Lord Astor said vibrantly: "I invited Lady Selsdon to dinner this Saturday evening. Is that okay by both of you?"

Baron Astor said: "Yes, Lloyd. Lady Selsdon is very welcome!"

Baroness Astor said lovingly: "Son, of course she is welcome! I will like to spend some time with my future daughter-in-law!"

Lord Astor continued and said enthusiastically: "I am meeting with her parents for dinner this Thursday evening to officially ask them for approval for their daughter's hand in marriage. I am bringing her here to both of you on Saturday so that you can approve our union!"

Baron Astor said happily: "Son, If you love her and she loves you, then, you have my approval!"

Baroness Astor added lovingly: "Lloyd, you have found a gem in Lady Selsdon! I approve of your union!"

Lord Astor said gratefully: "Thank you mom and dad!"

They all finished eating. Baron Astor and Baroness Astor retired to the study while Lord Astor went upstairs to his quarter.

At about 8.45pm, on the same Monday, Lord Astor was getting ready for bed when Lady Chelsea called him. He picked up the call.

Lady Chelsea said provocatively: "Good evening my Lord! How was your weekend?"

Lord Astor answered demurely: "Good evening Lady Chelsea. My weekend was busy. How was yours?"

She responded seductively: "It was an awful weekend! I was lonely. You were not there to fuck me! I was missing you terribly!"

Lord Astor said pitifully: "I am sorry my Lady!"

Lady Chelsea noted that he did not suggest how he intends to make amends to her. She said suggestively: "You will have to make it up to me! You will have to plan a whole week for me and take me on vacation or to a hotel and fuck me every day for the whole week!"

He responded reservedly: "We will see on Tuesday."

She was a little bit annoyed because he did not support or made any comment on her suggestion. She said annoyingly: "Darling, you did not comment on my suggestion. Can I start seeing you today and throughout the week?"

He responded and said: "No, not tonight. Tomorrow evening at 5.30pm. I will be at your place."

She knew something was amiss! This is not the usual Lord Astor that she was used to. Normally, he will be excited to come and sleep with her.

She said worriedly: "Did I do something wrong, my Lord! You sound aloof!"

Lord Astor said: "No, my Lady, I am just tired."

She did not believe him. She sensed something was wrong. Was it a new woman?

She pressed him further and said nervously: "My Lord, please tell me if I wronged you!"

Lord Astor knew he has a problem in his hands. It is going to be difficult breaking their relationships.

He responded and said: "You did nothing wrong my Lady. I will see you tomorrow."

She said: "Ok, my dear."

They hung up and went to sleep. Albeit, Lady Chelsea was troubled and had a bothered sleep.

It was Tuesday, and Lord Astor went to his office as usual. He left his office at about 5.00pm and drove towards Lady Chelsea apartment. He dreads what he is about to do to Lady Chelsea. It is pitiful but unavoidable. He got to her apartment and pressed the buzzer on her door.

Lady Chelsea opened the door feeling apprehensive. She went towards him and kissed him and said: "Good evening, my dear!"

Lord Astor said warmly: "Good evening, Chelsea."

They walked together into her living room and sat close together. She knew there was trouble! He did not carry her to her bedroom and make love to her.

She said: "Are we going out to dinner or are we eating in?"

He answered pitifully: "No, my Lady. There will be no dinner today."

He wanted to get it out quickly and reduce the drama. He said sorrowfully: "We cannot see each other as a couple again! I am ending our relationship!"

It was as if a thunder struck her! She knew something was wrong from yesterday. It was a female intuition!

She tried to make a play for it and see if she can salvage the situation. She inquired lovingly: "Have I wronged you?"

He replied and said: "No. I told you that before. You are a perfect Lady. You are a good Lady."

She continued worrisomely: "Then, why don't you want me? Is it another woman?"

He answered regrettably: "Yes. It is another woman that I love dearly. You did nothing wrong. I was not in love with you. I tried, but it just wasn't there. Please, forgive me, my Lady!"

She started sobbing and, then, crying out loudly. Lord Astor tried to comfort her by holding her in his hands, but she pushed him away.

She sobbed for a while and her eyes became red. Then, she said: "I thought you cared for me and was fond of me, and eventually you will fall in love with me. You did not give us a chance!"

Lord Astor was sorry for her and said compassionately: "I am fond of you my Lady. In fact, very fond of you! But, I do not love you like that. If we had continued and get married, you will eventually hate me, and we will get a divorce. It is right to break up now. You are an extremely beautiful woman, and eventually, you will find love and someone that loves you back!"

Lady Chelsea was still extremely perturbed and said annoyingly: "Lord Astor, please leave my apartment!"

Lord Astor said apologetically: "Please understand. Let's not be enemies."

She got up and walked him to the door. And as he stepped out, she closed the door behind him with no hugs or goodbyes!

Lord Astor was sad, but, knew he had to do it. At dinner, that night, he was morose. The parents asked him what was bothering him.

Lord Astor said: "I just broke off with Lady Chelsea this evening at her apartment. It did not go down well with her. I hope we will not become enemies!"

Baron Astor said compassionately: "I am sorry to hear that. It was for the best. After a while, she will get over it, even though, it is painful now."

Baroness Astor said sympathetically: "Yes, it is very painful for a woman. I feel empathy for her. Like your dad said, she will eventually get over it. Now, focus more on your bride-to-be!"

They finished eating dinner and Lord Astor went upstairs to his private quarter. He changed and put the telivision on. He sat down for a while and feeling very sorry for Lady Chelsea. She picked up the phone and called Lady Selsdon.

She picked up the phone and said: "Good evening, my betrothed! How was your day?"

Lord Astor responded sadly: "Not great!"

Lady Selsdon was concerned because she heard sadness in his voice. She inquired worriedly: "What is troubling you my Lord?"

He answered miserably: "I just broke off my relationship with Lady Chelsea and it did not go down well!"

Lady Selsdon felt relieved that the problem was not with her, but, nonetheless, was sorry for what transpired. She said: "I am sorry that she did not take it well. Such things happen and it is very painful for women. I hope she will be able to deal with it and move on. I am sorry for her."

Lord Astor said: "I feel sorry for her too. Well, how are you doing my love!"

She responded and said: "I was feeling well until you gave me the news."

He said: "Sorry to have bothered you. I had to tell you the truth!"

She said: "Thank you. I appreciate your candor! Are we still having lunch tomorrow?"

He answered hurriedly and reassuringly: "Definitely, yes. You know I cannot stay away from my Lady! Let's meet at the Connaught Hotel at 1.30pm. There is a fine restaurant in there that serves one of the best seafood in town. You will enjoy it!"

She responded and said eagerly; "That sounds good! Besides, you know I cannot wait to be in your company! I look forward to you holding me and kissing me passionately! I can't wait to see you tomorrow!"

He laughed out loud at her silly loving behavior and said: "My darling, the feeling is mutual!"

They said their 'good nights' and went to sleep.

It was Wednesday morning at about 12.00 noon as Lord Astor stepped out of his office and started heading towards the jewelers' shop. He got in and they showed him the engagement ring. It was extremely beautiful. It was placed in a white embroidery box and given to him. He was pleased with the diamond. He left the jewelers' store at about 1.00pm and drove towards the Connaught hotel. He arrived there at about 1.25pm and was given a seat by the host. He is well known by the host because he has been there several times with dates, and business lunches and dinners.

At about 1.30pm, Lady Selsdon arrived wearing a white skirt and navy blue blouse which matched her blue eyes. Her shape was alluring and she was looking royally beautiful! Lord Astor knew he was a lucky man! Her bride-to-be was a striking beauty! He got up and went to her, pulled her to himself, and kissed her passionately. Then, he let her go as the host took them to a seat by the windows.

They ordered seafood dinner and they started eating. A bottle of champagne was brought for them, which was part of a previous arrangement with the host by Lord Astor.

Lord Astor said delightfully: "Did you enjoy the seafood?"

Lady Selsdon said charmingly: "It is one of the best! I see you have good taste which you took from me!"

He laughed out loud and said: "Seriously! I thought you learnt it from me!"

She laughed and said amusingly: "My Lord, it is a Lady's prerogative to say that she is the one with the best taste and style, and not a man! So, accept what I said as a fact!"

He continued laughing and said lovingly: "You love a healthy debate! I see that I will have my hands full trying to win some arguments!"

She continued laughing also and said: "Somethings I will surrender to you willingly if you are very sweet to me!"

He laughed out loud and said: "I see that you are corrupt. Are you trying to bribe me? And what are you willing to surrender to me willingly?"

She giggled shyly and said: "Making good love to me!"

He laughed again and said jokingly: "You are a tease, my love!"

She said seductively: "Interesting! Let's see how sweet you are to me!"

He continued laughing and took the white box from his Jacket pocket and went to Lady Selsdon's side and knelt down by her side and opened the box. The diamond was big and sparkling. Virtually all the diners were looking and staring at them. Lady Selsdon was taking back and was not expecting it this soon. She has never seen a diamond this striking!

Lord Astor said affectionately: "Lady Astor, I asked again as a confirmation of my previous proposal: will you honor me by becoming my wife?"

The whole diners and waiters stood up and were shouting "Say Yes, Yes, Yes!"

Lady Selsdon stood up and yelled: "Yes. Yes, Lord Astor I will marry you!"

He slipped the ring into her fingers and stood up as he kissed her passionately, and she kissed him back passionately!

The diners and the waiters started hollering and clapping. They were laughing and cheering in support of the couple. At the same time, the host had huge bottles of champagne rolled in by the waiters, which was compliment of Lord Astor. The waiters started serving all diners free champagne.

Lord Astor went back to his seat as Lady Selsdon sat down. She raised her fingers up and examined it. She appreciated the diamond. She thought: "This is real! I am really getting married! Wow!"

Lady Selsdon said appreciatively: "Thank you, my love! I love you so much! I will be a good wife and make you happy!"

He smiled and said pleasantly: "I know my dear. I love you so much too! I will be a good husband to you!"

They finished eating lunch and went back to their separate offices. Lady Selsdon purposefully put her fingers in her jacket to ensure that her office staff is not aware that she is engaged. It is not time to tell them. Not yet!

However, He will show it to her family tonight and to her girlfriends tomorrow. She left her office at about 4.30pm and head towards home full of excitement! What a day!

At 7.00pm, Lady Selsdon came downstairs to join her family for dinner.

Lady Selsdon hid her fingers by her side as she sat down. She said excitedly: "Good evening everyone! I hope everyone had a great day!"

Baroness Selsdon said warmly: "Good evening daughter! I had a great day!"

Baron Selsdon said calmly: "Good evening Elizabeth. My day was routine. Nothing special!"

Olivia said sincerely: "My day was busy. My boss gave me too much tasks today. Good evening!"

Jane said tenderly: "Good evening Beth. Like dad, my day was routine!"

They started eating and making small conversations.

Then, Lady Selsdon got up and flashed her huge diamond ring on her fingers and shouted animatedly: "I am engaged! Look at the engagement ring that Lord Astor gave me today at Lunch!"

The ring was flawless and stunning as it sparkled in the light! Baroness Selsdon, Olivia and Jane got up and came close to Lady Selsdon to examine the ring. Then, they all hollered and laughed as they celebrate with Lady Selsdon.

Baroness Selsdon said enthusiastically: "Congratulations Elizabeth! It is time to start planning for a wedding!"

Olivia said happily: "Lizzy, I am happy for you! It is actually happening!"

Jane said gaily: "Wow, Beth! I am going to a wedding! My sister's wedding! Wow! Congratulations!"

Baron Selsdon came close to her daughter and hugged her. He smiled and said: "Congratulations my dear! I am happy for you!"

They all finished eating and went to their various quarters feeling very merry!

Lord Astor called Lady Selsdon and they spoke for about one hour before they went to sleep.

It was Thursday morning and Lady Selsdon went to work as usual while wearing non-see-through gloves to cover her ring from her staff. At about 12.00 noon, Lady Selsdon left her office and head to lunch to a restaurant across from the Mayfair Gallery of Bridal Group, Inc.

As she got into the restaurant, she saw that her friends were already seated and was taken to their table.

The ladies were excited to see one another.

Lady Selsdon said animatedly: "Good afternoon Ladies! I am famished! Let's eat!"

Lady Adetutu said gaily: "Good afternoon Elizabeth! Let's eat and go across the street!"

Lady Bhatia said vivaciously: "Good afternoon my Lady! Let's have some fun!"

Lady Andrews said merrily: "Good afternoon Elizabeth! I am ready to have some fun!"

Lady Ashton said animatedly: "Good afternoon Elizabeth! Let's eat so that I can pick your wedding gown!"

They started eating and drinking wine, and making small conversations. But, they found it odd that Lady Selsdon was eating with her gloves on. It was as if she was reading their minds! She got up suddenly and removed her gloves and flashed her new engagement diamond ring!

They all got up and started hollering, laughing, clamoring and clapping! They started singing "ring around the roses" and "She is taken and spoken for!" All the diners joined in the singing. As they were singing, they kept examining the ring which was sparkling in the lights.

Lady Selsdon said elatedly: "I am engaged! Lord Astor gave me the ring yesterday at lunch!"

Lady Andrews said congratulatory: "Congratulations, you fine wench!"

Lady Ashton said in a laudatory message: "My Lady, congratulations! Let's go get ready and plan the best wedding in London!"

Lady Adetutu said in a complimentary tone: "Elizabeth, what a week! You got engaged in less than two weeks! Wow! Congratulations, my Lady!"

Lady Bhatia said happily: "Lady Selsdon, congratulations! What colors are you choosing for your wedding?"

Lady Adetutu interjected and said elatedly: "My Lady, how about navy blue to match your beautiful blue eyes!"

Lady Selsdon said agreeably: "I agree Lady Adetutu. My colors will be blue for the bridal train and, stripped grey suit and blue ties for the men."

They all agreed on the colors and finished eating. Then, they went across the street into the Mayfair Gallery of Bridal Group, Inc. As they walked in, they were greeted and ushered in by Kyle Walker and David Bradley, President and vice-President of the group respectively. The Ladies were introduced to Joan Robert and Barbara Smith who are directors of garment designs and location designs respectively. They were told that they are in good hands and they intend to give them a wedding experience that they will never forget! Also, he told them that they do travel to their various offices worldwide, and if they have a plan for a wedding, they should give them a two-week head-start.

The Ladies examined various garments and, told Kyle and David that they will be back within two weeks to conclude on a wedding. Then, they left for their different homes.

Chapter 9:

The Affair at 45 Park Lane

It was still Thursday, and Lady Selsdon has just left his friends at the Mayfair Gallery of the Bridal Group, Inc. at 4.30pm. She drove straight to her parents' home in Belgravia. She went upstairs and dressed in casual pants and blouse as she awaits the arrival of Lord Astor.

At about 6.30pm, Lord Astor called Lady Selsdon and told her she was on her way to see her parents. Lady Selsdon went downstairs and joined her family in the study and they made small conversations.

At exactly 7.00pm, Lord Astor pressed the buzzer and was shown in by the butler to the study room. Lady Selsdon got up and went to him and kissed him in the mouth. The other family members got up to greet him.

Lady Selsdon said excitedly: "Mom, dad, Olivia and Jane, it is my pleasure to introduce Lord Astor, my fiancée, to you!"

Lord Astor came closed to them and shook all their hands.

Lord Astor said warmly: "Good evening Baroness Selsdon. It is my utter pleasure to make your acquaintance!"

Baroness Selsdon said affectionately: "The pleasure is all mine! It is good to meet with you!"

Lord Astor turned to Baron Selsdon and said: "My Lord, good evening! It is an honor to meet with you and be invited to your gorgeous house!"

Baron Selsdon said tenderly: "Good evening Lord Astor! Thank you for appreciating my abode. You are welcome to my house!"

Lord Astor continued and said: "I believe you are Olivia? It is great being in the presence of such a fine lady!"

Olivia said animatedly: "Thank you my Lord! Your words are kind!"

Lord Astor, then, turned to Jane and said kindly: "And, definitely, you must be Jane! Elizabeth did not tell me that her house is full of beautiful Ladies!"

Everyone laughed. Then, Jane said generously: "My Lord you are very rich with words! Thank you for the compliments!"

Baron Selsdon said: "Please come in and sit down while we wait for dinner to be served."

They all sat down as Lady Selsdon sat close to Lord Astor. Lord Astor has something to say, but was a little bit nervous. Baron Selsdon sensed his dilemma and helped the young gentleman broke the ice.

Baron Selsdon genially: "Lord Astor, I appreciate the acquisition of our company last week. My Chief Financial Officer just called me late this afternoon that your bank has transferred the funds to our account! I have not had the chance to share with my family yet! Thank you!"

Lord Astor said amiably: "My Lord, we should be grateful to you for trusting us enough to allow us to acquire your company! With you all retaining ten percent of the company, I will have double opportunities to spend quality time with Elizabeth!"

Seeing that an opening has been created for him, Lord Astor said entreatingly: "Baron Selsdon and Baroness Selsdon, as you are aware, I have fallen in love with Elizabeth and she has told me that she share the same sentiment with me. We have been spending some time together and our love has deepened with this past week. I cannot wait any longer. Therefore, I am kindly asking for your daughter hands in marriage and I need both of your approvals!"

There it is! It is out in the open! It is official!

Baron Selsdon said fondly: "Lord Astor, my daughter has told me that she is in love with you and that you want to marry her. You know she is dear to my heart and I know you will treat her well. You have shown to me that you are a responsible gentleman and, as such, you have my approval to marry Elizabeth!"

Lord Astor said gratefully: "Thank you my Lord. I will endeavor to make her very happy!"

Baroness Selsdon said lovingly: "Son, you have my approval! I can see that both of you are in love and I will not get in the way. Let me know what we can do to make your union comfortable!"

Lord Astor said appreciatively: "Thank you, my Lady! I will do as per your suggestion."

Not to be left out of the big occasion, Olivia inquired excitedly: "When is the date for the wedding? I want to go out and buy the finest dress I can lay my eyes on!"

Lord Astor said cordially: "I will work on a date with Elizabeth. I am thinking that four weeks from now, around the last Saturday of July, will be my choice if Elizabeth approves of that date!"

Lady Selsdon said agreeably: "Last Saturday in July is agreeable to me!"

Jane said enthusiastically: "Great! We have a date. It is time to start planning!"

Olivia inquired and said: "Lizzy, what is your chosen color?"

Lady Selsdon said: "Navy Blue for the bridal train and, stripped gray suits and navy blue ties for the men."

Baroness Selsdon interjected and said: "We need to start planning since we have very short time. There has to be location chosen, engagement announcements, and wedding planners chosen. I will seat with Elizabeth, Olivia and Jane to make the choices."

Lord Astor said: "Thank you my Lady!"

At that time, dinner was announced. They had a great dinner filled with small conversations, merriment and laughter. At about 9.00pm, Lord Astor took his leave and was escorted out by Lady Selsdon. It was a very happy Thursday night at the Selsdon's home. They all eventually retired to their private quarters.

As Lord Astor got home and changed into his pajamas, Lady Selsdon called.

He picked up the phone and said lovingly, and teasingly: "My love, I see you cannot get enough of me!"

Lady Selsdon said playfully: "Seriously, my Lord! You have not even started putting anything in me for me to get enough of you!"

Lord Astor laughed and equally playful said: "I can guarantee that when you start receiving, you will be too full and will beg me to reduce my deposit in you!"

Lady Selsdon laughed out loud and enjoying the moment, said friskily: "Flattery my Lord! Just Flattery! You will be put to the test shortly! I hope you can make it happen!"

Lord Astor laughed and said teasingly: "I will show you what I am made of shortly!"

Lady Selsdon said excitedly: "My love, I called to tuck you in bed and request to know where we are meeting for dinner tomorrow?"

Lord Astor said lovingly: "Darling, I enjoy your company a lot! You are full of taste, color and spicy flavor! Let me pick you up from your apartment at 6.00pm and we will drive to 45 Park Lane for dinner. I maintain a penthouse suite there for my getaway. We may spend the night there if you chose!"

Lady Selsdon giggled and said: "It sounds enticing! I will pack a night bag so that we can spend the night together!"

It was music to Lord Astor's ears. He said indecently: "I thought you were too timid to be in my private space!"

Lady Selsdon laughed and said: "You are just a big and lovable teddy bear!"

Lord Astor laughed and said: "Ok my Lady! I will pick you up at 6.00pm. Good night my love!"

Lady Selsdon said lovingly: "Good night darling!"

They hung up and went to sleep,

It was Friday and Lady Selsdon was in her office. At about 10.00am, Lady Selsdon's friends called and wanted to go to lunch with her. They placed her on a five-way conference call.

Lady Selsdon picked up the phone and said warmly: "Hello Ladies! What's up?"

Lady Bhatia said elatedly: "Good morning my Lady! We called to see if we can do lunch and then go hang out in your apartment tonight?"

Before Lady Selsdon could respond, Lady Ashton interjected and said: "Yes, that will be fun and we can help you plan your wedding and list of invitees for your engagement and wedding!"

Lady Selsdon said appreciatively: "Thank you for the suggestion. But, I cannot do lunch and dinner today."

Lady Adetutu said disappointedly: "Oh no! That would have been a lot of fun! Why can't you do it?"

Lady Selsdon understandingly: "I know, Lady Adetutu. It would have been fun. However, I have a previous date with Lord Astor for dinner tonight and tomorrow night. Let's move our lunch date and hang out night to next Tuesday. Is that ok by everyone?"

All the ladies agreed that it was okay by them.

Then, Lady Andrews said naughtily: "Interesting! You will be having dinner dates for two nights! Wow! That means you going to be fucked over and over for forty-eight hours! Ouch! You are going to be feeling very raw!"

They all laughed!

Lady Selsdon responded mockingly and said: "Yes, Lady Andrews, I want him to fuck me well for forty-eight hours! After all, your boyfriend does more to you and we do not complain!"

The ladies busted out laughing!

Lady Ashton added teasingly and obscenely, and said: "At least Lady Selsdon is tight down there, and hers is not like yours which is a deep canyon that a man can drive a trailer through!"

All the Ladies started hollering on the phone and laughing uncontrollably!

Then, Lady Selsdon interrupted and said pragmatically: "On a serious note, Lord Astor came yesterday and officially asked for my hands from my parents, and they gave us their approvals to go ahead and wed. Tomorrow, I will be officially introduced to his parents and seek their approvals for us to get married!"

Lady Andrews said excitedly: "Wow! It is really happening Elizabeth. You beat us to the altar! I am going to read the riot act to my boyfriend that if he does not put a ring on my finger within a month, then, I will close my legs tight!"

The ladies started laughing again.

Lady Adetutu said sarcastically: "Lady Andrews, please stop that drama! You know you are a nymphomaniac and you are incapable of keeping your legs close!"

All the ladies started hollering on the phone again and laughing irrepressibly!"

Lady Selsdon interrupted the jesting and said: "We have decided that we should wed on the last Saturday of July! So everyone keep your calendar open and reserve that date for me. In addition, we will discuss details more when we meet on Tuesday."

Lady Ashton said warmly: "Great job Elizabeth! I am very happy for you, my Lady!"

Lady Bhatia said: "Congratulations Elizabeth! We will mark our calendars and see you next Tuesday. Please text us the place for lunch for next Tuesday."

They all hung up the phone after saying their 'good byes'.

At about 4.00pm, Lady Selsdon left her office and head towards her apartment at Kensington Place so that she can prepare for his date with Lord Astor. She notified her parents that she will be with Lord Astor and will see them on Sunday.

She got home and took a bath and packed a night bag. She said to herself: "Lord Astor, you though I am frigid! Well, I am going to wear you down tonight! I am hotter than a volcano! I am virtually your wife! Bring it on my fine gentleman!"

She put on a lilac bra and panties, and a loose lilac dress. She put on her diamond ring and some perfume and was ready for her naughty rendezvous with her betrothed! At about 6.00pm and as she left her bedroom, the door to her apartment buzzed. She opened the door and saw Lord Astor. She thought: "Damn! He was a handsome devil! A hunk of a man!" She was suddenly very wet and hoped to be laid by him right there!

She said weakly and teasingly: "My love, you looked damn fine! What is the occasion?"

He laughed and said mockingly: "You look damn beautiful yourself, darling! The occasion is a dangerous liaison with my wife! What are your beguiling thoughts this evening, my Lady?"

She giggled and said: "A dangerous liaison! Hmmm! I should be very scarred!"

He laughed more and said raunchily: "Do not be scarred, madam! I will be very gentle on my Lady!"

Lady Selsdon said seductively: "We will see! Shall we go now?"

They got in Lord Astor's navy blue Aston Martin and drove towards 45 Park Lane Hotel. He parked and they checked in as Lord and Lady Astor! Then, they took the elevator up to the penthouse suite. He opened the door and went into one of the most luxurious suite that Lady Selsdon has ever seen!

She walked into the master bedroom and placed her night bag in one of the closet and said: "Darling, it is a very extravagant suite!"

He said: "Yep! I like the luxury and attention to details. Are we eating in or going downstairs?"

She said cheekily: "I put on this elegant dress for my husband and I want to be seen in his hands and show off my diamond! Call me shameless! Let's go downstairs and eat so that I can be seen by people with my husband!"

He laughed out loud and tried to kiss her, but she ran away and said: "Not now love! You will ruin my lipstick!"

He kept laughing and said: "Ok! Let's go eat!"

They went downstairs and were taken to a private section of the restaurant. They decided to eat an Italian meal plus red wine.

Lord Astor said charmingly: "What are you going to do now that my executives will be in control of your company within three weeks!"

Lady Selsdon said teasingly: "You are my husband! What should I do? Stay home and become a house Lady or move to your office?"

He laughed and said: "My Lady, I do not see you as a housewife! You will be bored stiff!"

She giggled and said playfully: "Really! I may not be bored if you keep me busy on my back and pump me with babies!"

He laughed out loud and said brazenly: "Darling, you are just impossible! Keeping you busy on your back every day will send me to an early grave!"

She laughed too and said salaciously: "I do not want that! I need my husband! I need to keep you alive for a long time so that you can make love to me every day for the next 70 years!"

He busted out laughing and said: "Woman, you have dangerous wits! I intend to make love to you every day for the next 70 years and keep you very happy!"

She continued to giggle for a while and said seriously: "Lloyd, let me remain as the executive vice-chairwoman of Agar Pharmaceuticals and when the babies start arriving, then, I can mix motherhood with executive-hood!"

He said agreeably: "Ok! I sanction your proposal!"

Then, their food was served and they started eating.

Lady Selsdon placed one of her legs on the lap of Lord Astor under the table where no one can see what she was doing! He pulled the leg more to his lap and tickled her toes. She giggled out loud!

He smiled and said wickedly: "My Lady, you are scandalous! Is it your intention to make love to me here in public?"

She giggled more and said depravedly: "Are you scarred? Because I can feel your erection here under the table in public!"

He laughed out loud as he was enjoying the moment with her bride-to-be! He said cravingly: "I am not scarred my Lady! Rather, I am more energized to please you extremely! Emphasis on extremely!"

Lady Selsdon started laughing hysterically and said iniquitously: "Seriously! Do not blame me my Lord because you brought this heat on yourself! I am going to make you beg me for mercy!"

Lord Astor continued to laugh irrepressibly and said spicily: "Darling, you will have to put up or show up!"

Still laughing, she said delightfully: "Lloyd, you know I love you a bunch!"

He said adoringly: "Elizabeth, I love you a bunch my darling!"

They finished eating and decided to go upstairs. She put her leg down and got up as he came around and kissed her passionately. Then, they walked out together as she put her hand into his elbow. They rode the elevator up as he held her close to himself

As they got into the penthouse suite, he closed the door and kissed her passionately and carried her to the master bedroom. He took off his own clothing. Then, he took off all her clothes including her bra and underpants. She lay naked looking extremely beautiful, and looking up at him in a tantalizing manner!

Lord Astor looked at the naked body of Elizabeth and wicked desire shut through his body as he became erect with an enormous manhood! She saw his erection and she became extremely wet with intoxicating desire. He pushed her legs open and entered her forcefully. She shouted in ecstatic pleasure and moan as he kept thrusting into her in rapid manner. She kept wriggling under him as he kept pounding away into her. Her body was shaking in rhythmic pleasure as she was enjoying his forceful thrust. He was extremely enjoying his bride as he kept the tempo going on for over thirty minutes! He pulled out of her and turned her around and entered her from the back. He started pounding her from behind forcefully and kept thrusting rapidly into her as she was having orgasmic pleasure. After another thirty minutes of love making, they both reached a cataclysmic and intoxicating climax!

He pulled out of her and had her lay in his hands as he pulled her close to himself. They were exhausted and inebriated as if drunk with hard liquor!

Lady Selsdon has never had such spellbinding sexual pleasure! She said lasciviously: "My Lord, that was extreme and intense! What were you doing to me?"

He thoroughly enjoyed their love making and was the best sexual experience he ever had! He laughed and said indecently: "You brought it on yourself, my love! You wanted extreme and you got it!"

She started laughing and said seductively and teasingly: "Please my Lord, have mercy on your fragile subject!"

He started laughing frenziedly: "Ok, my dear! I will show mercy!"

They laughed and conversed playfully into the night. Then, they made love again and fell asleep as they rested throughout the whole night.

They got up late in the morning at about 9.00am. Then, he made love to her again for over forty-five minutes. At about 10.00am, they got up and took showers together.

As they got out of the shower, he tried to make love to her again, but she ran away from him and said playfully: "Not now darling! I am hungry and starved! You promised to feed me and fatten me for the kill! What happened?"

He kept laughing and said enticingly: "Elizabeth, you are too hilarious and you could kill me with your subtle wits!"

She was laughing too and said lovingly: "My dear, please order room service so that I can have a decent breakfast."

He said: "Okay."

Then, he ordered room service. They watched the news on television as they wait for their meals. About twenty minutes later, their breakfast was brought up and laid out in the living room.

They ate and rested for a while. Then, he made love to her again for another forty-five minutes. After which, they fell asleep. They got up at about 4.00pm.

Lady Selsdon said: "We need to get up, and off this bed in the next thirty minutes and get ready to go have dinner with your parents.

He said: "You are right, my love!"

At about 5.00pm, they started getting ready. They left the hotel at about 6.00pm and drove to One Grosvenor Square.

They arrived at the Astor's residence at about 6.30pm and were shown to the study by the butler since they were being expected.

They walked into the study and Lord Astor said warmly: "Good evening mom and dad! Please meet my fiancée, Lady Selsdon!"

Baron Astor and Baroness stood up to greet them.

Lady Selsdon said tenderly: "Good evening my Lady, and my Lord! It is a great honor to meet with you!"

Baron Astor said affectionately: "Good evening, Lady Selsdon! It is a pleasure to meet with the beautiful Lady that has captured the heart of my son!"

Lady Selsdon said kindly: "Thank you my Lord! That was very kindheartedly of you!"

Baroness Astor said amiably: "My dear Lady Selsdon, you are welcome to our home! You are an extremely beautiful woman! My son has made a great choice! Please come and sit down next to me and maybe your beauty will rub on me and make me as beautiful as you!"

Everyone busted out laughing!

Lady Selsdon said sweetly and lovingly: "My Lady, you are so sweet and modest! Your elegance and beauty is very striking, and I should be the one begging that your beauty should rub on me!"

Everyone laughed again!

Baroness Astor said lightheartedly: "Lady Selsdon, I see why my son fell in love with you and why I know I will fall in love with you as if you are my real daughter!"

They all sat down and continued conversing.

Then, Lord Astor said warmly: "Mom and dad, you know that I have already proposed to Lady Selsdon and she has already accepted. I saw her parents this past Thursday and I officially asked for their approval to marry Lady Selsdon. That approval was given. I, now, ask you, mom and dad, to extend the same approval to our intended union!"

Baron Astor said affectionately: "Lloyd, I have met Elizabeth and I am enthralled with her intelligence, beauty, and poise. You all have my approval!"

Lord Astor and Lady Selsdon said in unison: "Thank you my Lord!"

Baroness Astor said lovingly: "You both have my approval!"

Lord Astor said: "Thank you mom!"

Lady Selsdon said appreciatively: "Thank you my Lady!"

Lord Astor added: "We are looking at the last Saturday of July for our wedding. That means that we need the list of your invitees within a week so that we can send out the invitations immediately!"

Baroness Astor said agreeably: "I will get my secretary to draw up the list by Tuesday and get it to you that evening. Let's go and eat!"

They all got up and went to eat. Dinner and more conversations were completed by 8.00pm. After dinner, Lord Astor and Lady Selsdon left One Grosvenor Square and drove back to 45 Park Lane Hotel.

Chapter 10:

Lady Selsdon and Friends at Knightsbridge

At about 8.30pm on Saturday evening, Lord Astor and Lady Selsdon arrived back at 45 Park Lane Hotel and took the elevator up to his penthouse suite. As they got into the suite, Lord Astor closed the door and started kissing Lady Selsdon overpoweringly. He lifted her up and carried her to the master bedroom, and gently lay her down on the bed.

He first of all took of all his cloths and stood naked before Lady Selsdon as she observed and examined his physique, his strong erection and huge manhood. She was again extremely wet with lustful desire. He came closed to her and gentle pulled off her dress, and her black bra and panties. As he came close to her, she put her hands on his chest and raised herself up to kiss him.

He lifted her of the bed, parted her legs and thrust into her forcefully. Lady Selsdon shouted out loud as she felt his enormous manhood entering her body. She started moaning louder as he kept thrusting into her over and over for over forty minutes. She became delirious with orgasmic pleasure as he kept pounding at her.

He, then, pulled out of her and carried her to the dresser and turned her around so that her face was looking into the mirror and can see what he is doing to her. While standing up behind her and bending her over the dresser, he penetrated her again from the back. She looked into the mirror and saw him entering her over and over again, and she started having wild erotic fantasies of their lovemaking. He was taking her breath away and kept pounding into her for another thirty minutes until both of them had an earth-shattering orgasmic climax.

He pulled out of her and carried her to the bed, and laid her down gentle. Both of them lay down side by side tired and spent.

Lady Selsdon knew that this love-making was exceptional as her body was still shaking from several intoxicating orgasms.

She got her breath back and said dirtily: "At this rate, I will not be able to walk down the aisle with you! My legs are shaky and if you keep doing this to me, I will start walking funny and people with notice that there is something wrong with my gait!"

He laughed out loud and said raunchily: "Such a scandalous language from a refined Lady that should not be uttered in high class and civilized society, my Lady!"

She laughed frenziedly and said salaciously: "What you just did to me cannot be uttered in high-class and civilized society because it will get you expelled from civil society, my Lord!"

His laugh became hysterical and he said shamelessly: "But, you told me that you want me to be extreme! Is my fine Lady begging me to tone it down?"

She took the pillows and threw it at him playfully and said raunchily: "I am not scarred of your extreme love making! I am capable of controlling the beast in you!"

He continued to laugh and said excitedly: "My Lady, you are impossible!"

She changed the subject and said: "I need your list of invitees by Tuesday evening plus your mother's list so that we can send out the invitation letters by the following Friday. That will give the guests three weeks to prepare. In addition, this coming Friday at about 11.00am, I will make a reservation for us, your friends, and my friends at the Mayfair Gallery of the Bridal Group, Inc. so that we can finalize their appointment as our wedding planner."

He agreed and said: "You are right my love! I will email you the list. I will put the date on my calendar. Also, tell your friends that I am inviting them to a society wedding for next Saturday. It will be a forerunner of our own wedding."

She said: "Ok. I will tell them. Just text me the address so that I can forward it to them and coordinate their arrival with ours. Also, after the meeting at the gallery next Friday, let's come here to this penthouse suite and not wait till evening to come here. I will pack my night bag and the clothing for the wedding of your friend next Saturday."

He said mockingly: "That is good by me! I see you can't wait to get more pounding from me in the early afternoon instead of at late night!"

She laughed and threw a pillow at him and said spicily: "Do not flatter yourself, my Lord! It is just logistics!

He laughed and said sardonically: "Yep my Lady! Logistics? Or wanton desire?"

They both laughed and continued to trade banter and make small conversations till late in the night before they fell asleep.

At about 7.00am on Sunday morning, she woke him up and said he needs him to get up and go drop her off at her apartment because she has to drive to her parents' home to go to church with them. They got up, took a shower and dressed. They left at about 8.00am and he drove her to her apartment where they agreed to talk later tonight.

After dinner and at about 8.30pm, Lady Selsdon called her friends and put them on a five-way conference line.

Lady Selsdon said warmly: "Good evening my fine Ladies!"

Lady Ashton said kindly: "Good evening Elizabeth! What is trending in your intelligent brain?"

Lady Selsdon said: "A lot!"

Lady Adetutu said: "Good evening my Lady! Please share."

Lady Bhatia said: "Good evening Elizabeth! Tell me something exciting!"

Lady Selsdon said: "I have a lot of exciting things to share with you Ladies if I can just get it out!"

Lady Andrews said tawdrily: "Good evening Elizabeth! We know you spent the whole weekend with Lord Astor which I bet is the exciting news you have to tell us! Or how he finally made you a fucking nymphomaniac! That is fucking exciting!"

All the Ladies laughed irrepressibly!

Lady Selsdon said indecently: "Yes, Lady Andrews, I was fucked very well throughout the weekend! And, yes, he made me a fucking nymphomaniac! Yes, I enjoyed it thoroughly! And, yes, please do not be jealous!"

The ladies started hollering, laughing and clapping on the phone!

Lord Bhatia said temperedly: "Ouch! Too much X-rated information! Can you all keep your racy sexual encounters private and to yourself?"

All the Ladies Laughed again!

Lady Adetutu said admonishingly: "Lord Bhatia, stop being a prude! You fucked everywhere and pretend as if you have never been fucked hard!"

The ladies started laughing again uncontrollably and hollering!

Lady Ashton interjected and said rebukingly: "Ladies, please calm down and let's hear what Elizabeth has to tell us!"

Lady Selsdon said thankfully: "Thank you Lady Ashton! Firstly, I am inviting everyone to a wedding of one of Lord Astor's friends scheduled for next Saturday. I will text you the address and mail the invitations to you all by Tuesday. I will also coordinate our arrival time with yours."

She paused and continued: "Secondly, we all, including Lord Astor and his friends, will meet next Friday at 11.00am at the Mayfair Gallery of the Bridal Group, Inc. to finalize location, list of invitees, entertainment, food, and choice of garments."

She paused again and continued: "Finally, my engagement to Lord Astor will be held two Saturdays from now, and is for close friends and family only. I will text you venue details by Tuesday. Phew! That is a lot of activities in two weeks!"

Lady Andrews mimicked her and said: "Phew! Elizabeth, that is a lot! But, I am game and ready for everything!"

Lady Ashton said warmly: "Great, Elizabeth! Count me in! I will be there for all the events and intend to have a good time!"

Lady Adetutu said: "Elizabeth, that is exciting! I will be there for all the events!"

Lady Bhatia said: "Count me in too my Lady! I agree it is going to be exciting and I will be looking very elegant!"

Lady Selsdon said gratefully: "Thank you my Ladies. Do not forget that we are having a sleepover at my place on Tuesday and we will discuss these events more!"

Lady Adetutu said: "That sounds good! So we are cancelling lunch and coming to your place at about 5.00pm?"

Lady Selsdon said: "Yes that is the plan. See you all at 5.00pm on Tuesday!"

They all said 'Good night' and hung up!

On the same Sunday, at about 9.00pm, Lord Astor called his friends to give them some information.

Lord Astor said happily: "Good evening fine fellas!"

Lord Adeniyi said lively: "Lloyd, I see that you are very happy! That looks like a man that has been vagina whipped!"

The friends laughed out loud!

Lord Astor said agreeably: "You are very accurate! I am in love!"

More laughter from the friends!

Lord Anderson said indecently: "We know you are in love! But, we also know that you are in love with the vagina whipping that your Lady gave you!"

All the friends hollered and laughed frenziedly!

Lord Ahmad said dynamically: "Good evening Lord Astor. What are you real excited about?"

Lord Astor said gratefully: "I have lot of information I want to share with you guys!"

Lord Alton interrupted and said sprightly: "A lot of information is not what is making you this happy as if you are on a drug! You must have had a very good time this weekend with your fiancée that is making you so joyous!"

Everyone laughed again!

Lord Astor said patiently: "My Lords, will you all let me present the information?"

Lord Ahmad said agreeable: "Ok, friends, let's give him a chance to finish."

Lady Astor said appreciatively: "Thank you Lord Ahmad! I am inviting you all to a wedding of one of my friends scheduled for next Saturday. I will text you the address and send the invitations to you all by Tuesday. I will be coming with Lady Selsdon, and I will coordinate our arrival time with yours."

He paused and continued: "You all, including me, Lady Selsdon and her friends, will meet next Friday at 11.00am at the Mayfair Gallery of the Bridal Group,

Inc. to finalize location, list of invitees, entertainment, food, and choice of garments."

He paused again and continued: "Thirdly, my engagement to Lady Selsdon will be held two Saturdays from now, and is for close friends and family only. I will email you the venue details by Tuesday. Are we all on board with these activities?"

Lord Alton said warmly: "I am all in! I have no new girlfriend. So, I may I come alone and actively looking for love!"

They all Laughed!

Lord Astor said supportively: "Lord Alton, we can arrange a date for you! But, I cannot guarantee that you will fall in love with her!"

There was more laughter!

Lord Anderson said sincerely: "I have my own beautiful girlfriend who I will bring to the events. We are getting very tight and I may propose to her after Lord Astor's wedding!"

They all cheered and hollered!

Lord Astor said tenderly: "Great Lord Anderson! We will stand with you whenever you are ready!

Lord Ahmad said happily: "I also have a betrothed Lady that I will bring to all the events. I will be there to support you!"

Lord Astor said gratefully: "Thank you Lord Ahmad!"

Lord Adeniyi said indigently: "I will surely be there, my Lord. I have no date to bring! The Lady I met at the Ascot is not interested in commitment! All she wants is for me to be her fucking machine!"

All the friends started hollering and laughing over the phone!

Lord Adeniyi continued: "I intend to chat up Lady Adetutu, Lady Selsdon's friend, to see if she can have me. She is very beautiful and I will like to make her mine! Lord Astor, can you ask Lady Selsdon if she is available?'

Lord Astor said comfortingly: "I will ask her tonight and text you whatever she tells me."

They discussed more and bantered around before they said their 'Good night'.

At about 10.00pm, Lord Astor called Lady Selsdon. She picked up the phone.

Lady Selsdon said jokingly: "Whatever you want: the answer is 'no'!"

He started laughing irrepressibly!

Lord Astor asked teasingly: "My love, what do you think I was going to ask?"

Lady Selsdon laughed out loud and said mockingly: "That I should come to your place right now and be fucked!"

He laughed frenziedly and said: "My Lady, I will love that, but I will not burden you with such pleasures tonight!"

She laughed more and said: "Burden of pleasure is not welcome till next weekend!"

He responded while still laughing and said: "Yes my dear. My request is for Lady Adetutu. My friend, Lord Adeniyi, wants to know if she is available because he is interested."

She said replied and said: "Yes, she is available. I will inform her of his interest and text her number to you to forward to him, once I get her approval!"

He said: "Ok, darling. Good night!"

She responded and said: "Good night, my love!"

They went to sleep.

It was Tuesday and Lady Selsdon decided to leave her office at 3.30pm and head to her apartment at Kensington Place to await the arrival of her friends. Her Mother has sent her list to her. Lord Astor and her mother have sent the list of their invitees by email to her. The number of guests for the wedding has skyrocketed. She got home, took a shower and changed into casual clothes. At about 5.00pm, her friends buzzed her apartment door. She opened the door.

Lady Selsdon said sparklingly: "Hi ladies! Come on in."

They all went in as the ladies took their night bags to different bedrooms. Then, they all dressed into casual clothing and joined Lady Selsdon in the living room.

Lady Selsdon said casually: "Before we order dinner, I need Lady Adetutu to give me permission to send her phone number to Lord Astor to forward to Lord Adeniyi. He is enchanted with you!"

Lady Adetutu said: "Ok. Send it to them. I saw him last time at the Polo match and I did fancy him! He is a handsome hunk. I will date him and hope he just doesn't want to fuck me and move on!"

The Ladies started laughing!

Lady Selsdon said: "Ok, I will send it now. Lady Adetutu, be optimistic! He may be falling in love with you already! Give him a chance."

All the Ladies agreed and shared the sentiment of Lady Selsdon.

Then, Lady Selsdon said: "What should we order for dinner?"

Lady Ashton said: "I have a taste for Chinese cuisine. Are we game?"

All the Ladies agreed and Lady Selsdon ordered the meals as she took their various orders.

Lady Selsdon said animatedly: "I have not received the guest's list from you Ladies for my wedding. I have received from my Mother, Lord Astor and Baroness Astor. What happened to you lovely wenches?"

Lady Andrews said: "I just emailed my list now!"

Lady Bhatia said: "Sorry for the delay, my Lady. It is ready, but I wanted to discuss it with you first so that the number of guests will not be overcoming! But, I just emailed it to you now."

Lady Selsdon said appreciatively: "Thank you Lady Bhatia! That is very thoughtful. If the number becomes overwhelming, then, we will erase some guests off the list!"

Lady Ashton said: "I share the same thought with Lady Bhatia. My guest list is large. I just sent mine now. If it is too much, then, let me know and I will revise it now."

Lady Selsdon said: "Let's look at the whole figure and if it is overwhelming, then, we will curtail it!"

Lady Adetutu said: "I have the same issue with everyone else! I just emailed my list also."

Lady Selsdon continued and said: "Let me go get my laptop and correlate the whole list and see what numbers we have."

As she went to get her laptop, their meals were delivered. They placed all the different orders on the dining room table and they sat down and started eating.

Lady Selsdon opened her laptop and correlated the list. She exclaimed and said: "Wow! The total guests on the list is about 850 people! Wow! My fiancée will kill me!"

The ladies laughed and told her to trim the number below whatever they are comfortable with. They were prepared to trim theirs right away!

Lady Selsdon said: "Let me call Lord Astor now and find out what his opinion is on this number!"

She dialed his number and he picked up the phone immediately.

Lord Astor said amorously: "Hello my love! What ails you?"

Lady Selsdon responded and said lovingly: "Hi darling! What ails me is the number of guests everyone wants to invite to the wedding! I am here with my friends and planning all details of the wedding. As of now, the guest list is 850 people! What number should we trim it down to?"

He responded delightfully: "I enjoyed lunch yesterday! I can't wait to see you for lunch tomorrow!"

She responded adorably: "My Lord, I enjoyed you too at lunch yesterday. Please tell me what number to trim this 850 people to!"

Lord Astor said: "I like it! I wanted a big wedding and I got it! It is my dream to have a huge wedding in London! Leave it at 850 people! Do not trim it!"

Lady Selsdon was flabbergasted and said: "You like the number! You want me to keep the 850 people untrimmed?"

Lord Astor said: "Yes! And I will see you for lunch tomorrow. I will text you the restaurant that we are going to later tonight!"

She said: "Ok, my love! Bye!"

They hung up the phone.

Lady Andrews said raunchily: "Aha! We caught you in the act! What ails you is the fact that you wanted to be fucked tonight as you were fucked yesterday during lunch!"

The ladies laughed!

Lady Selsdon said: "Lady Andrews, I did not get fucked yesterday because all I did was eat lunch. And, today, I am here with you Ladies!"

They all giggled!

Lady Ashton said: "Elizabeth, please ignore Lady Andrews. So where are we?"

Lady Selsdon said: "You all heard him! There will be no trimming of the guests' list! We are going to work with 850 guests!"

Lady Adetutu said happily: "That is good by me!"

Lady Bhatia said: "Alright! Let's work with this number!"

They finished eating and started planning the wedding details. They worked throughout the night and went to bed shortly before midnight. They woke at about

7.30am and dressed hurriedly as they Left Lady Selsdon's apartment and went to their various offices.

It was Wednesday morning at about 11.30am and Lady Selsdon looked at her text from Lord Astor to confirm the address of the restaurant for their lunch date. The text said: "Let's meet at 1.00pm at the Bancone Restaurant near Knightsbridge".

She was being driven by the chauffeur in the Bentley and they left the office at about 12.30pm. They arrived at the restaurant at exactly 12.58pm. The chauffeur stepped out and opened the door for Lady Selsdon. She went in the restaurant and saw that Lord Astor was already waiting for her in the lobby. He got up and went towards her, hugged her and kissed her on the lips passionately.

He said lovingly: "Hi darling! Good afternoon!"

She responded adoringly and said: "Good afternoon my love!"

The hostess took them into a very private section of the restaurant. They ordered steak dinners and red wine.

Lord Astor said affectionately: "How was your day? I know you all were very busy planning the wedding last night. How did it go?"

Lady Selsdon said lovingly: "Still busy! We have compiled all the guests' list and at 850 guests, that is huge! Do you seriously want all that guests?"

He answered and said: "Yes my love! I want all the guests. I want a big wedding!"

She said: "We will need a venue that is big enough for all that guests!"

He responded and said: "We will find the right venue. Do not worry about that."

He continued and said: "Actually, I know a very fine venue: The Dartmouth House in Mayfair."

She responded knowingly and said: "I know that venue! Yes, that is great! Let's use it!"

He said alluringly: "That is settled. Now, I need my wife! Can you come to my place tonight?"

She laughed and said seductively: "Why? What do you want?"

He laughed and said provocatively: "I want to make love to you!"

She laughed and said teasingly: "I do not need extreme tonight! I am tired from planning last night. Besides, I am still recovering from last week pounding!"

He laughed and said jokingly: "I will not be extreme tonight! I will be as gentle as a dove!"

She continued laughing and said playfully: "I do not want you to be gentle! I enjoyed your extreme love making! But, not tonight! Let's wait till Friday since you will have me from the early afternoon and through the weekend! It gives me something to look forward to!"

He said lovingly: "Ok, darling. I will wait till Friday!"

They ate their meals and left the restaurant at about 2.45pm.

Chapter 11:

Wedding Plans at the Mayfair gallery of Bridal Group, Inc.

It was Thursday evening at 9.00pm, after dinner at the Selsdon' house. Lady Selsdon just finished having dinner with her family and changing into her pajamas. She decided to call her friends on a five-way conference line.

Lady Selsdon said: "Good evening, Ladies!"

Lady Adetutu said inquiringly: "Good evening Elizabeth. What is up?"

Lady Selsdon replied: "I am just ensuring that you Ladies should not forget we are all meeting at the gallery tomorrow."

Lady Ashton said: "Elizabeth, we have already put that date on our calendar. We got your back! We will be there!"

Lady Selsdon said appreciatively: "Thank you Lady Ashton!"

Lady Bhatia said sleepily: "Lady Selsdon, I am going to sleep. Is there any other information you want to share with us!"

Lady Selsdon said teasingly: "Are you going to sleep at 9.00pm? Or is your boyfriend there with you and you have other plans?"

Lady Bhatia responded lively: "Yes, my boyfriend is with me and we have to do grown people things!"

Lady Andrews interjected and said unabashedly: "Stop being a prude Lady Bhatia! You are going to be fucked by your boyfriend! Just say it! It is not a banned word in the English language!"

The Ladies laughed!

Lady Selsdon interrupted and said understandingly: "I understand Lady Bhatia. Let me just discuss one more item and I will let you go enjoy yourself!"

Lady Andrews continued and said sleazily: "Let her go continuing fucking and we will give her the information later!"

The Ladies giggled!

Lady Selsdon ignored Lady Andrews's remark and said: "I have just texted everyone the address of the wedding for this Saturday. Also, the colors chosen by the bride is turquoise? Please find something in that range or add to your accessories."

Lady Adetutu said appreciatively: "That is a beautiful color. I just checked my phone and I got the text for the location. We are meeting you all there at 11.00am, right?"

Lady Selsdon said approvingly: "Yes, you are correct. Also, for the following Saturday, which is my engagement, the color to wear will be white."

Lady Ashton said: "That is a good color for the engagement. Also, I may have to go shop for something in turquoise!"

Lady Bhatia said impatiently: "I got it!"

Lady Selsdon said: "Ok, Ladies, that is it. I will see you all tomorrow. Good night!"

They all said 'Good night' and hung the phone.

At about the same time on Thursday, Lord Astor was on a five-way conference line with his friends.

Lord Astor said jovially: "Hi fellas! Just checking on you guys to confirm our meeting at the gallery tomorrow at 11.00am."

Lord Adeniyi said: "Good evening, Lord Astor! We will be there. Do not be anxious!"

Lord Astor said jokingly: "Anxious? No, I am not. Just informational!"

Lord Anderson said: "Good evening my Lord! I may come with my girlfriend!"

Lord Alton said jokingly: "I am coming by myself!"

The friends laughed!

Lord Ahmad said: "I will be there, my Lord!"

Lord Astor added and said: "Also, the color chosen for the Saturday wedding of my friend is turquoise. You all can wear turquoise ties. I already emailed you the address."

Lord Alton said: "It sounds good. I will be dressed to impress and see if I can find me an elegant Lady to hang on my hand!"

The friends laughed!

Lord Adeniyi added jovially: "Thank you Lloyd for the phone number of Lady Adetutu! We have been chatting every day. I am having lunch with her tomorrow after the meeting at the gallery. Also, I asked her to accompany me to the wedding on Saturday and she agreed! So, I am good!"

Lord Astor said approvingly: "Great Lord Adeniyi! I am happy for you!"

Lord Alton said: "Great! I will see you all tomorrow."

Lord Astor said: "Thank you guys! Will see you all tomorrow. Good night!"

They all said 'Good night' and hung up the phone.

It was Friday morning at 10.00am and Lady Selsdon decided to call Lord Astor. He picked up the phone.

Lord Astor said tenderly: "Good morning darling! Are you getting ready to leave your office?

Lady Selsdon said lovingly: "Good morning Lloyd. Yes. I will be leaving in about thirty minutes. I called to tell you that you should wait for me till I get there so that we can go into the gallery together."

Lord Astor said agreeably: "Ok, dear. I will wait for you. Were you able to confirm the appointment with the gallery for today?"

Lady Selsdon replied and said: "Yes. I called them on Monday and we have a confirmed appointment for today."

Lord Astor said: "Ok. I will see you shortly."

They hung up the phone. At about 10.30am, Lady Selsdon left her office and was driven by the chauffeur in the Bentley. They drove towards the Mayfair Gallery of Bridal Group, Inc.

Also, at about the same time, Lord Astor was in the back of his Roll Royce being driven by his chauffeur. They got to the Mayfair Gallery before Lady Selsdon. He saw her coming and got out to meet with her. They kissed and walked into the gallery together.

In the lobby of the gallery, Lord Astor's friends and Lady Selsdon's friends were already seated. They all got up to welcome Lord Astor and Lady Selsdon as they all exchanged greetings. As they all walked in, they were greeted and ushered in by Kyle Walker and David Bradley,

President and vice-President of the group respectively. Then, they were all introduced again to Joan Robert and Barbara Smith who are directors of garment designs and location designs respectively. Again, they were told that they are in good hands and they intend to give them a magical wedding experience that will be the talk of the town!

Kyle took everyone to a designing table and they all sat down to discuss details. Two secretaries joined them to take notes. Kyle started the meeting by welcoming them and having everyone introducing themselves to the group.

Kyle said congratulatory: "Lady Selsdon and Lord Astor, congratulations on your big day! What date have you chosen?

Lady Selsdon said warmly: "Kyle, I will let Lord Astor answer all your questions!"

Lord Astor said: "We have agreed to be wed on the last Saturday of July."

Kyle said warmly: "That is a good day! The weather is beautiful and warm!"

Then, he continued: "We can provide location or you can give us a chosen location and we will handle all transactions on your behalf. Do you have something in mind?"

Lord Astor replied and said: "We have chosen the Dartmouth House in Mayfair. You can meet with them immediately. I have reserved the venue and paid to use it for Friday for your preparations and on Saturday for the wedding."

Kyle responded and said: "Great! That is settled. Venue is a very important component of any wedding plan."

He continued and asked: "What are the colors for the wedding?"

Lord Astor replied and said: "Navy blue for the bridal train and stripped grey suit for the groom train plus navy blue ties for the men."

Kyle said: "Wonderful! What do you have in mind for live bands?"

Lord Astor responded and said: "We need a versatile live band that can play all sort of music that ranges from calypso, reggae, blues, to rock and roll! I want it to be a happy occasion!"

Kyle said: "That is noted. What are we looking at in terms of guests? Large number of guests or close friends and family members?"

Lord Astor replied and said: "I want a big wedding that will be the talk of the town! We are inviting 850 guests!"

Kyle smiled and said: "Magnificent! We need all the guest names and addresses ASAP!"

Lord Astor looked at Lady Selsdon to answer that part of the query.

Lady Selsdon said: "I will email the guests' names and addresses to you immediately we conclude our meeting today. This way the invitations will be mailed out by next Tuesday!"

Kyle responded and said: "I have the staff to do that! We will get it out by Tuesday! We will show you different designs to choose from before you leave."

Lady Selsdon added and said: "Also, I have a second list for the engagement which contains 50 guests of close family and close friends only. That is for the following Saturday at the Four Seasons Hotel in Mayfair. Please, get those invitations out by Monday. This will be the official announcement for the engagement and wedding!"

Kyle responded and said: "Very good! We will make it happen!"

He continued and inquired: "Are you all ready for the garment fittings today? So that you all can choose the design for the garments."

Lord Astor said: "Yes we are here to be fitted right away!"

Kyle said: "I have all the information I need. If I need anything else, I will call Lady Selsdon and Lord Astor to provide such information for me."

He continued and said: "Ladies and Lords, please follow Joan Robert and Barbara Smith who are our directors of garment designs and location designs for garment fittings so that you all will be well-fitted."

Then, he addressed Lady Selsdon: "Please my Lady, go with David to choose all your designs for your gown, bridal gowns, cakes, and invitation letters. Then, you will be fitted by Joan Roberts."

Then, Kyle addressed Lord Astor and said: "Lord Astor, I will have the total costs ready soon. I will give it to you and you can discuss this with you bride and get back to me by Monday."

Kyle Stepped into his office and did some calculations and came back to join Lord Astor.

He said: "The total costs of the wedding will be $3.5 million. I have placed everything in this envelope!"

As he gave the envelope to Lord Astor, he said: "Lord Astor, please go and get fitted now."

Lord Astor said: "Thank you Kyle!"

At about 2.00pm, and after fittings, everyone started exiting the gallery while exchanging greetings and promising to meet tomorrow, Saturday, at Lord Astor's friend wedding. Lord Adeniyi and Lady Adetutu left together. While, Lady Selsdon told Lord Astor to pick her up from her apartment at Kensington Place in about two hours because she has to go to her parents' home to pack a night bag.

Lady Selsdon was dropped off at her parents' home in Belgravia by her chauffeur at about 2.30pm. She went in and saw that her parents were in the study. She narrated all that transpired at the Bridal Group, Inc. today. Also, she told them that she will be spending time with Lord Astor and they have a friend's wedding to attend tomorrow. She said 'Good bye' to them and went upstairs to take a shower and get dressed for her date with Lord Astor. She wore a loose wine-colored flowery dress, and underneath that, she wore wine-colored underwear. She packed a night bag with clothing items for the dinner and wedding. She left at about 3.30pm and drove her red Jaguar Sports towards her own apartment at Kensington Place.

She got there at about 3.50pm and went in. At exactly 4.00pm, Lord Astor buzzed the door and she opened the door. He stepped closed to her and kissed her.

He pulled back and said: "You look smashing, darling! Can we go?"

She said: "You too, my love! Yes. Let's go!"

They drove towards 45 Park Lane Hotel in his navy blue Aston Martin and parked. They took the elevator up to Lord Astor's private penthouse Suite and went in.

Immediately they got into the penthouse suite, Lord Astor could not wait for Lady Selsdon to drop her night bag. Instead, he closed the door and kissed her passionately and carried her to the master bedroom. She dropped her bag on the floor. He took off his own clothing. Then, he took off all her clothes including her wine-colored bra and underpants. She lay naked looking seductive and enticing. She looked up at him longingly as desires welled up in her! She was having lascivious thoughts and erotic cravings!

Lord Astor looked at the naked body of Elizabeth and naughty cravings shut through his body as he became erect with a massive manhood! She saw his erection and she was instantly wet with inebriating desire. He pushed her legs open and entered her powerfully. She bellowed in rapturous pleasure and groan as he kept thrusting into her with quick tempo. She was writhing under him as he kept hammering away into her. Her body started quivering in episodic pleasure as she was enjoying his vigorous thrust. He was tremendously relishing his lovemaking with his bride as he kept the tempo going on for over one hour! He pulled out of her and turned her around and entered her from behind. He started hammering into her from behind powerfully and kept thrusting rapidly into her as she was having orgasmic pleasure. After another twenty minutes of love making, they both reached an earth-shattering and mind-altering climax!

He pulled out of her and both of them lay side by side. Then, he pulled her close to himself. They were exhausted and fell asleep.

They got up at about 7.30pm and were starved. They decided to order room service for dinner. Dinner comprised of various seafood items like shrimps, crab cakes, and baked cod.

As they started eating, Lady Selsdon was still relishing the thought of their lovemaking. She knew that their lovemaking gave her hypnotic sexual pleasure! She said beguilingly: "Lloyd, were you deprived of sex when growing up? I need to psychoanalyze you to understand why you enjoy extreme and intense sexual play!"

Lord Astor laughed frenziedly and said: "You are going to psychoanalyze me because I enjoy sexual pleasure with my bride-to-be? Wow, my Lady! That is an extreme mindset darling!"

He continued laughing and said lewdly: "No darling, I was not deprived! Maybe my Lady, I should psychoanalyze you, sweetie, why you thoroughly enjoyed lovemaking with me that is extreme and intense! Were you deprived of sexual pleasure all this time?"

She laughed uncontrollably and said cheekily: "My Lord, it is not fair for you to copy my thoughts! It is called plagiarizing for your information! Besides, because I enjoy lovemaking with you should not give you license to enjoy flattery on my behest!"

He continued laughing irrepressibly and said brazenly: "You are impossible my dear! You have a mastery of words that I cannot compete with! I concede! You are going to kill me with laughter!"

She continued laughing wildly and said: "Just continue to be extreme so that I can become your sex slave! That is what you want! To condition my body to be craving your lovemaking! I know what to do to you."

Lord Astor, still laughing, said provocatively: "My love, I have never enjoyed any woman like I do you! Please do not blackmail me by making me a lap dog that cannot function until I see you!"

She hollered and laughed out loud. She said salaciously: "Now, I know you are not a gentleman, my Lord! Gentlemen of fine upbringing do not lie or try to deceive the one they love! You probably tell all your previous girlfriends the same crazy line!"

He laughed again and said: "Enough of this banter! I am coming after you now!"

He got up and made a play for her. She ran away from him and said naughtily: "Get away from me you depraved sex freak!"

As they ran around the living room, there was a knock at the door for room service. Dinner was delivered and they sat down together to eat their meals.

As they were eating, Lady Selsdon said lovingly: "Lord Astor, I love you a bunch!"

He smiled and said affectionately: "Lady Selsdon, you make me very happy! I love you a bunch and a bunch!"

She giggled and said: "Thank you darling!"

He laughed and said: "You are very welcome my dear!"

They continued to banter and conversed playfully into the night. At about 10.30pm, he started making love to her again. Thirty minutes later, they fell asleep and rested throughout the whole night.

It was Saturday morning at about 8.30am and he got up trying to make love to her again, but she pushed him away and told him they will be late for the wedding if they do not get ready immediately. He agreed and they went and took showers together.

At about 10.00am, they were ready. Lady Selsdon was wearing a tight hugging dress in turquoise with a flowery turquoise hat. She was looking extremely gorgeous with a shape-to-die-for! Lord Astor was wearing a grey suite, white shirt under it and a turquoise tie. He was looking extremely debonair. They looked good together and they knew it!

They got into his navy blue Aston Martin and drove towards North Hampstead for the wedding between Lord Islington and Lady Camden. As they arrived at the venue, they saw a lot of guests being ushered into the venue. They parked and walked towards the entrance.

Besides the entrance gate, they saw their friends already waiting for them. They were all well dressed and looking lovely.

Lord Alton said warmly: "Good morning Lady Selsdon and Lord Astor. Both of you looked fine together!"

Lady Selsdon and Lord Astor said sincerely together: "Thank you Lord Alton!" Then, Lord Astor continued and said: "You look swell yourself"

Lord Anderson said: "Fine morning to both of you! Please meet my girlfriend, Lady Sutton!"

Lady Selsdon and Lord Astor said amiably together: "It is a pleasure to meet you Lady Sutton, and of course Lord Anderson!"

Lord Ahmad and her date exchanged greetings with Lady Selsdon and Lord Astor.

Then, Lord Adeniyi said tenderly: "Wow, what a fine couple! Good morning my Lord and Lady. Please meet my date, Lady Adetutu, whom you already know!"

Lord Astor said amiably: "Thank you my Lord and Lady! Both of you are extremely gorgeous couple too!"

Lady Andrews and her date shook her hands with Lady Selsdon and Lord Astor, and they all exchange pleasantries. Lady Ashton came with no date and exchange greetings with everyone.

Lady Bhatia came with her fiancée and both were dressed in traditional Indian clothing in turquoise. They both exchanged pleasantries with Lady Selsdon and Lord Astor, and with all the friends in the group.

Lord Astor said to his group: "Please, let's all go in. I was told that all my friends have been placed on the same table."

So the whole members of Lord Astor's group went in and were shown to their table. The wedding ceremony of Lord Astor's friends was just starting. There was pomp and pageantry. The venue was decorated in splendor and the live band was playing beautiful music. There was gaiety, laughter and merriment. The guests were enjoying themselves as they mingled and converse. The gentlemen were flirting with the women and everyone was having a good time. The atmosphere was magical!

The wedding ceremony of Lord Islington and Lady Camden, including the reception came to an end at about 6.30pm. All the friends and their dates exited the venue shortly after exchanging 'Good byes' to each other. Lord Astor and Lady Selsdon drove back to 45 Park Lane Hotel and went up to the penthouse.

Again, unable to control himself, and as they entered the penthouse, Lord Astor closed the door behind them and kissed Lady Selsdon passionately. He undressed her right there in the living room. Then he lifted her up against the wall and penetrated her while he was still standing. He kept making love to her for about twenty minutes. Then, he pulled out of her and carried her to the bedroom. He took off all his clothes and was standing naked before her as she examines his masculine body.

Lady Selsdon looked at his manhood and wicked desires exploded in her body again as she became extremely wet again. She saw that his manhood was erect, big and throbbing. All she wanted was him to enter her. He got close to her and pulled her thighs apart and thrusted into her. Lady Selsdon moaned loudly as she felt him penetrating her forcefully. He increased the rhythm of his thrust as she kept raising her hips to absorb the power of the force behind the penetration. They were both making loud noises as the pleasure of their love making overwhelmed both of them.

He kept making love to her for another one hour until they were consumed and drained. He pulled out of her and laid side by side with her.

It was about 9.00pm and both of them fell asleep and slept the whole night.

They woke up at about 7.30am. He pulled her close to him and started kissing her.

Lady Selsdon said affectionately: "I have to go to church! You have to go drop me now!"

Lord Astor replied and said amorously: "I know! But, I want you now!"

She responded and said: "Not now darling!"

He said alluringly: "Just for some minutes!"

He kept kissing her as she responded to his kissing and touches.

He pulled the bed sheet cover away from her and made her bend over the pillows with her tummy and face lying on the bed. He raised her buttocks up and parted her legs. He entered her from behind as she groaned loudly with pleasure. He continued banging hard into her in a recurrent tempo for over forty minutes. Lady Selsdon's pleasure reached an orgasmic crescendo that her legs became weak as both climaxed together.

He pulled out of her and she got up from the bed. But, as she started walking towards the bathroom, her legs were weak and shaky as she staggered like a drunk with pure pleasure to the bathroom. Lady Selsdon's body was still shaking with rhythmic pleasure that she has to sit down on the bathroom stool.

He came close to her and held her to himself. He said worriedly: "Are you okay, dear?"

She responded weakly: "Yes, I am fine. I just need to catch my breath!"

He was still troubled and said: "Do you want to rest a little bit?"

She looked at the time. It was 8.20am. She replied and said: "No, dear. Let's both take showers and, then, you have to go and drop me so that I will not be late for church with my family."

He responded and said: "Ok darling!"

They finished taking showers and dressed hurriedly. He drove her to her apartment and promised to give her a call later tonight.

Chapter 12:

The Engagement at the Four Season Hotel, Park Lane

It was 9.00pm on the same Sunday evening. Lord Astor made a phone call to Lady Selsdon. She picked up the phone.

He said lovingly: "Good evening my Lady! How are you doing?"

She responded mockingly and said: "Good evening my darling! Aha! Are you checking on me to see if I need a doctor to fix my damaged body?"

He laughed out loud and jokingly: "On the contrary my love! I was checking to see if you need more of my amorous services!"

She laughed and said teasingly: "Seriously! I am going on a one month hiatus from your services, my Lord!"

He busted out laughing and said: "Please my love, don't do that! It will literally kill me!"

She continued laughing and said: "I forgot to tell you that I did transfer all the guests' information to the Bridal Group, Inc. before you picked me up on Friday. He told me that the engagement letters will go out on Monday and the Wedding invitations will be sent out by Thursday!"

He responded and said: "That is great. Also, I will deliver a check to him for $3.5 million first thing tomorrow morning so that there will be no delay. Then, I will come to dinner tomorrow and discuss with your dad about the bill. Please inform him in advance so that I will be welcomed for dinner."

She said: "Ok, I will. Also, we will not have lunch tomorrow because I have a meeting with all members of my staff to formally inform them of the successful acquisition. So, let's shelve our lunch date to Wednesday at 1.00pm. Please text me as usual where we are meeting for lunch. I am going to sleep now. Good night dear!"

He responded and said: "Ok, I got it and I will text you our restaurant for Wednesday lunch. Good night my beautiful one!"

She laughed as he hung up the phone.

It was Monday morning and Lady Selsdon was already in the office at 9.00am. She has two announcements to make to all members of staff of Agar Pharmaceuticals. Emails were sent to all members to log on to the company Zoom account at exactly 10.00am today.

At exactly 10.00am, all members of staff logged into the company's Zoom account. They were able to see Lady Selsdon in her office as she started the meeting.

Lady Selsdon said lively: "Good morning ladies and gentlemen. I want to show appreciation to all members of staff of our great company, including executives, managers, and line staff. Thank you."

She paused as the staff acknowledges her gratitude.

She continued and said: "On behalf of the Chairman and the Board of Directors, I have been authorized to inform you of their appreciation of the great work everyone has been doing for this company, especially for the successful acquisition. Before, I share what I was authorized to tell you, I have my own personal announcement to share."

Lady Selsdon paused and continued elatedly: "It is with pleasure that I announce my engagement to Lord Astor!"

The whole members of staff clapped and started hollering with joy. Their merry sentiment is based on the fact that virtually all employees of the company love Lady Selsdon because she has been polite, respectful and good to them. They actually love her!

Lady Selsdon raised up her fingers so that they can see the engagement ring with the sparkling diamond. There were thunderous applauses and 'Congratulations' from everyone.

She continued and said: "Thank you all for your cheerful sentiment. My secretary will send out emails to everyone to announce the engagement and the wedding date."

She waited for the merry sentiment and applauses to die down before continuing on the second announcement.

Lady Selsdon paused before saying excitedly: "My second announcement comes directly from the Chairman and the Board of Directors of our company. I have been authorized to inform you that, with the acquisition, everyone job is safe and guaranteed. There will be no layoff. In addition, everyone will get a big bonus ranging from $100,000 to $1.00 million depending on your level in the company! It means the minimum bonus is $100,000!"

There was pandemonium on the company's Zoom account as all the employees started hollering, clapping and laughing uncontrollably! The clatter and noise of appreciation continued for nearly ten minutes! They were all saying 'Thank you, Lady Selsdon!"

Lady Selsdon, eventually, raised her hands for quiet. She said: "You are all welcome. We appreciate you and we are proud of the work you all are doing here. Thank you and good morning!"

As she dismissed the meeting, another pandemonium broke out as the workers continued to holler and clap with joy!

Lady Selsdon left her office early at about 4.00pm to have a meeting with her parents before Lord Astor arrives for dinner. She was driven home by her chauffeur in the Bentley. There was a little traffic and they got home at about 4.45pm.

She went in and saw that her parents were in the library and watching television and conversing. Surprisingly, Olivia and Jane were there too.

Lady Selsdon said warmly: "Good evening parents! Good evening Olivia and Jane! Hope everyone had a good day! And, Olivia and Jane, why are you home early?"

Baroness Selsdon said tenderly: "Good evening Elizabeth! Yes, I had a great day. Thank you."

Baron Selsdon said affectionately: "Good evening my daughter! I know you have a lot to share!"

Lady Selsdon said lovingly: "Yes dad, I have a lot to share!"

Olivia interrupted and said: "Good evening Beth! It is not early. I just got home before you did."

Jane added and said: "Good evening Lizzy! Yes, I left early today. I got home at about 4.00pm."

Lady Selsdon said warmly: "Great! I am glad that you all are here. I have a lot to share!"

She paused and continued as she addressed her dad: "Dad, I did what you told me to do. I inform all our employees that the Board has approved that everyone will get a bonus from the acquisition from a minimum of $100,000 to $1.00 million."

Baron Selsdon said: "Great!"

Baroness Selsdon said inquiringly: "How did they take it?"

Lady Selsdon laughed and said: "There was pandemonium as they all hollered with joy. Dad, that was very benevolent of you! You made them happy! I also told them there will be no layoff due to the acquisition!"

Baroness Selsdon said happily: "I am glad we got a chance to put smiles on their face!"

Olivia said inquisitively: "That is a lot of money to about 2,000 employees. Is it not, Beth?"

Before she could reply, Jane jumped in and asked curiously: "Where is that money coming from?"

Baron Selsdon said informatively: "It comes from part of the money that was paid to us from acquisition of the company. Elizabeth, what will be our hit!"

Lady Selsdon said: "About $350 million!"

Baron Selsdon said: "Not too bad!"

Lady Selsdon continued: "Dad and mom, Lord Astor will be joining us for dinner at 7.00pm. Is that okay?"

Baron Selsdon said: "Yes, that is ok."

Lady Selsdon continued: "The engagement invitations have been sent out today. The wedding invitations will be sent out by Thursday!"

Olivia interrupted and clapped. She said excitedly: "I am so happy for you Beth! It is happening!"

Jane interjected and said animatedly: "Yes, Lizzy! I can't wait to get dressed and enjoy your wedding!"

Lady Selsdon continued and said: "Mom, dad, Olivia and Jane, you all have appointment at the Mayfair Gallery of Bridal Group, Inc. on Wednesday at 11.00am for garments' fittings."

Baroness Selsdon said: "We will be there Elizabeth."

They finished discussions and, Lady Selsdon and her sisters went upstairs to their private quarters to take showers and get ready for dinner.

At exactly 7.00pm, Lord Astor arrived for dinner. Lady Selsdon went to greet him and ushered him to the study.

Lord Astor said jovially: "Good evening Baron Selsdon and Baroness Selsdon. Thanks for having me for dinner!"

Baron Selsdon said tenderly: "You are always welcome son!"

Baroness Selsdon said affectionately: "Good evening Lord Astor. You know you are now like a son to me! So, you are welcome here anytime!"

Lord Astor responded and said: "Thank you my Lord and Lady!"

Then, Lord Astor turned to Olivia and Jane and said: "Good evening Olivia and Jane. I am glad that I will be in the company of such elegant Ladies!"

Olivia said gaily: "You are welcome Lord Astor. Such fine compliments my Lord!"

Jane said vivaciously: "Thank you my Lord. For such nice compliments, I will seat on the other side of you at dinner so that I can pick your brain for fine words!"

They all laughed!

Baron Selsdon said nicely: "It is time for dinner. Without much ado, let's go to the dining room!"

They all proceeded to the dining room where all sorts of English cuisine were on the table. They were served dinner and they started eating.

Baron Selsdon said to Lord Astor: "I know you all have been planning the engagement and wedding with Baroness Selsdon and your friends, and I have been provided very little information!"

Lord Astor said apologetically: "I am sorry my Lord. It is not intentional. It is the bride's day and I have been flowing with what she desires. And, also because of the time constrain due to the quick wedding date, we have tried to fast track all preparations! My apology again. I will do better!"

Baron Selsdon said: "No problem. I was told that you all have finalized the transaction with the Bridal Group,

Inc. As the father of the bride, it is my duty to take care of those expenses!"

Lord Astor said agreeingly: "Yes, my Lord. Traditionally, it should be the case. But, with current views, the groom can now be part of the transaction."

Baron Selsdon said stubbornly: "I am still a conservative and a traditionalist. I will stick to the old role of Father of the bride!"

Lord Astor said in an ameliorate tone: "Yes, my Lord. I do agree with you. The issue is that Lady Selsdon wanted a small wedding list, but I wanted a big wedding list. And as such, I feel it should be my responsibility to bear the burden of such demand!"

Baron Selsdon said: "I am okay with a big wedding. But, it does not negate the fact that I still want to take responsibility!"

Baroness Selsdon interjected to bring harmony to the dining room and said conciliatorily: "Let's mix tradition with modern and share the burden equally. This way, we will all be happy!"

Baron Selsdon said appeasingly: "That is fair! What say you Lord Astor?"

Lord Astor said propitiatingly: "I accept that proposal as fair my Lord!"

Baron Selsdon continued and inquired: "What costs are we looking at?"

Lord Astor said: "$3.5 million, my Lord!"

Baron Selsdon said: "Ok. After dinner, I will write a check for $1.75 million to you. Is that good?"

Lord Astor responded and said: "Yes, my Lord. Thank you for bending the rules for us!"

Baron Astor said: "You are welcome!"

Lord Astor looked at Baroness Selsdon and said: "Thank you my Lady for your wisdom!"

Baroness Selsdon said warmly: "You are welcome my son!"

They continued conversing into late at night. At about 10.00pm, Lord Astor took his leave and was seen to his car by Lady Selsdon. They kissed passionately before he drove off.

It was Tuesday night at about 9.00pm and Lady Selsdon has just gotten to her quarters after finishing dinner with her family. She decided to touch base with her friends. She called them on five-way conference line. The friends picked up the phone.

Lady Selsdon said lively: "Fine evening to you, my Ladies!"

Lady Andrews said curiously: "Fine evening to you Elizabeth. What are you excited about now?"

Lady Selsdon laughed and replied: "Lady Andrews you must be in a foul mood! It is the first time I have not heard you use salacious language! Are you okay?"

All the Ladies started laughing!

Lady Andrews said morosely: "My boyfriend travelled since last Sunday and will not be back till Friday, just a day before your engagement. I have not been fucked since then! I am lonely!"

All the friends busted out laughing!

Lady Adetutu said teasingly: "Lady Andrews, you must be a nymphomaniac! When Lady Ashton characterized you as such, I thought she was joking! I cannot believe that you are actually feeling depressed because you have not been fucked for three days! Wow!"

Everyone hollered and started laughing frenziedly!

Lady Ashton said comfortingly: "Lady Andrews, I do not know if this will help you. Take comfort that I have not been fucked for over nine months and I am not gloomy! Can you please control your hormones?"

The friends kept laughing uncontrollably!

Lady Selsdon said pitifully: "Lady Andrews, I know how you feel! He will be back in three days and you can eat him up then. But, for now, please chill out and be calm!"

Lady Bhatia said: "Lady Selsdon, what is it that you want?"

Lady Selsdon said: "I just want to remind you Ladies to go shopping for fine white clothing for my engagement this Saturday!"

Lady Adetutu said: "Relax my Lady. Do not be anxious! We will dress to kill for your engagement and for your wedding! Please be rest assured!"

Lady Selsdon said: "Thank you my friends! Good night!"

They all said 'Good night' and hung up the phone.

It was Wednesday afternoon at about 12.00 noon and Lady Selsdon looked at her phone and saw the text from Lord Astor. The text said: "Meet me at the Claude Bosi at Bibendum in West End at 1.0pm." She told her secretary to call her Chauffeur to be ready to leave at 12.30pm.

At exactly 12.30pm, Lady Selsdon's chauffeur opened the back door of the silver Bentley for her. They drove for about twenty-five minutes and arrived at the restaurant at about 12.55pm.

She got out of the Bentley and walked into the restaurant where Lord Astor was already waiting as usual. Always punctual! He came close to her and kissed her passionately.

The Hostess took them to a very private section of the restaurant. They ordered traditional French cuisine with white wine.

Lord Astor said tenderly: "Darling, please send my regards and gratitude to your mom for saving us on Sunday!"

Lady Selsdon said affectionately: "I definitely will. Have you paid Bridal Group, Inc.?"

He answered and said: "Yes, I did on Monday!"

She said: "Great! That is out of the way. Please tell your friends that the gallery said all the garments will be ready for collection the Friday after this coming Friday."

He said appreciatively: "Wow! They are very fast! I will pass on the message.

She added and said: "I will also notify my friends by text later tonight. Further, my family went to the gallery for fitting today. An appointment has been made for your mom and dad for garment for next Wednesday at 11.00am. Please kindly inform them."

He responded and said: "Thank you. I will notify them."

Their food arrived and they started eating. Lord Astor said amorously: "You know I missed you a lot, my dear!"

She said lovingly: "I missed you a lot too, darling! I long for you to hold me in your hands!"

He laughed and said: "Then, let's go to my apartment immediately after lunch!"

She laughed and said naughtily: "Seriously, my love! You must be kidding!"

He laughed and said provocatively: "Not kidding! I want you now!"

She kept laughing and said: "You are a tempter! And, a wicked one at that! You know I have a weakness for your touch and you try to manipulate me! It is not happening today, darling!"

He laughed and asked innocuously: "Why darling?"

She said innocently too and said teasingly: "Because, I have unfinished task at the office!"

He smiled and said cheekily: "Ok, I have to wait till Friday!"

She laughed out loudly and said tenderly: "It will not happen on Friday, either!"

He pretended to be morose and said: "Why not? We always meet on Friday!"

She said patiently: "True! You are correct! The only difference this time is that our engagement is this Saturday. And, it is not tradition for me to be humped the whole

Friday by my fiancée and get up in the morning and rush to my parents' home before coming to the engagement ceremony! My mom and dad will have a fit!"

He laughed and said reasonably: "You are right, my dear! My request is unreasonable! Let's focus on the engagement!"

She said agreeably: "Thank you my love for your understanding! However, after the engagement at 4.00pm, you can drive me to 45 Park Lane Hotel at your penthouse and be extreme with me!"

He laughed out loud and said alluringly: "My Lady, you are just impossible! It is a deal! I will be extreme! And, you can now refer to me as Mr. Extreme!"

She laughed out loud also and said seductively: "I cannot wait till Saturday to see you darling!"

He said: "We need to leave before we spend the whole afternoon here bantering!"

Lady Selsdon said inquiringly: "Before we leave, I have one more question. After our wedding, where shall we live?"

Lord Astor said warmly: "Interesting my Lady! I have been thinking about that for the past week and I actually got an Estate Agent to start a search for a home for us. And, I chose a nice one which I will take you to see next week. If you approve of it, then, I will purchase it immediately so that an interior decorator can work on it and finish it before we get back from our honeymoon!"

She was amused at his capacity to be forward planning at all times. She said appreciatively: "That is very sweet darling! Where is the location of the property?"

He replied enthusiastically and said: "It is in Belgravia and it is close to both your parents' home and my parents' home. This way, you will have support from both family members!"

She was happy with the decision and said gratefully: "Thank you my love! You are so thoughtful and caring!"

He smiled and said: "You are welcome my dear! It is befitting for a good human like you!"

She continued and asked again: "What is the cost?"

He replied and said: "$20.00 million!"

She said worriedly: "Is that not too expensive? We are young and we do not need such a big house!"

He answered calmingly: "We need it. We will grow into it!"

She said: "Ok."

They finished dinner and left the restaurant. Lady Selsdon went back to her own office, while Lord Astor went back to his own office.

It was Saturday morning and the day of the engagement ceremony. About fifty guests were expected for the observance of the preliminary announcement of the union. It should not last more than four hours. There will be a small live band. Only family members and close friends are expected.

At the Selsdon's home, everyone was getting ready and there was gaiety in the atmosphere. They all piled into the grey Bentley and were driven to the Four Seasons Hotel at Mayfair. They arrived at 10.55am. They got out and were taken by the hostess to a special cordoned off restaurant at the hotel.

As they approached the restaurant, they saw that Lord Astor and his family were already waiting for them.

They all exchanged pleasantries and were taken to the high table to be seated. All their friends and other family members were already seated.

The waiters and waitresses started serving food and various alcoholic beverages. Then, the live bands started playing various music by the Beatles and other pop artists. Then, the Master of Ceremony announced that the father of the bride wants to give a speech.

Baron Selsdon got up and started speaking lively: "My Lords, My Ladies, family members, and our friends! Today is a fine day. A fine day for my family. A fine day for the Astor's family. An extreme fine day for my daughter. And, an extreme, and extreme fine day for Lord Astor!"

He paused as they all cheered and applauded. Lady Selsdon and Lord Astor look at each other and laughed because only both of them knew the meaning they ascribed to the word 'Extreme'!

Baron Selsdon continued and gave a beautiful story of her daughter, Lady Selsdon, and the fact that she was a special gem for any fine gentleman. He finished his speech and sat down.

Then, the Master of Ceremony stood up and introduced the groom, Lord Astor.

Lord Astor stood up and started speaking excitedly: "How did I meet this gorgeous woman? It was at the Ascot Racecourse! It was as if I was struck by a thunderbolt! Or was it lightening that struck me?"

There was laughter and applause!

He continued and said: "I saw one of the most beautiful and stunningly elegant woman I had ever seen. It was love at first sight! Then, we spoke and I discovered that she was a very intelligent woman and the kindest soul I have ever known! Then, I knew I was in trouble! I was in love! And if she did not fall in love with me, then, I will have to live the rest of my life in abject misery!"

Everyone applauded and hollered as there were all laughing!

As he finished giving his speech, there were sparkles everywhere and flashes of 'Marry me Lady Selsdon!' Lord Astor went close to his bride-to-be and knelt down in front of her as he presented her with an engagement ring with a 7-carat diamond that was so beautiful that its brilliance dazzled everyone in the room. She took it and removed the previous one as she put on the new one. She got up and said: "Yes! I will marry you!" Then, they kissed passionately.

The crowd got up and they were all hollering, cheering, and laughing!

Then, they all got up and started dancing as they joined the newly engaged couple on the floor. The party ended at about 3.30pm as the guests were seen exiting the restaurant. Lady Selsdon was dropped off at her apartment at about 4.00pm by her family in the grey Bentley as she went in to await Lord Astor.

At about 4.30pm, Lord Astor arrived to pick her up and they drove together to 45 Park Lane Hotel. They parked and went upstairs to his penthouse.

Chapter 13:

The Wedding Location at Dartmouth House, Mayfair

Immediately they entered the penthouse, Lord Astor was feeling depraved with repressed cravings and quickly closed the door behind them as she kissed Lady Selsdon fervently. He undressed her as they head to the master bedroom. Then he lifted her up on to the bed and penetrated her immediately he laid her on the bed. He kept making love to her for about thirty minutes. Then, he pulled out of her and entered again from the side as he kept entering her rhythmically. He pulled out and took off all his clothes and stood naked before her as she inspects his masculine body.

Lady Selsdon surveys his manhood and naughty desires exploded in her body again as she became extremely wet again. She saw that his manhood was erect, big and throbbing. All she wanted was him to enter her. He got close to her and pulled her thighs apart and thrusted into her. Lady Selsdon moaned loudly as she felt him penetrating her powerfully. He increased the tempo of his thrust as she continued raising her hips in delight to absorb the power of the force behind the penetration. They were both making loud noises as the pleasure of their love making astounded both of them.

He kept making love to her for close to one hour until they were expended and exhausted. He pulled out of her and had her lay on his chest.

At about 7.00pm, he ordered room service for dinner. They got up from the bed and took showers. Then, they went to the living room as their meals were delivered.

Lady Selsdon said enticingly: "I will not be going to church tomorrow, Sunday. I told my mom that I will be with you. Is that okay by you?"

He laughed out loud and said tantalizingly: "Okay by me? You got to be kidding, darling! I am elated to have you here with me for the next two days!"

She laughed and said indecently: "So that you can be extreme with me, my Lord? Seriously?"

He laughed and said jokingly: "Yes, I will be extreme! But, frankly, my love, so that I can enjoy your company!"

She giggled and said teasingly: "Yeah, darling! You are excited like a child in a candy store! You are going to be greedy and eat all my candies!"

He busted out laughing and said indecently: "Madam Candy, I am going to extremely enjoy your candy!"

She said longingly: "Come over here my Lord and eat more candy!"

He got up excitedly and went close to her and said raunchily: "At your service, Madam Candy!"

But, as he was about to start playing with her, the doorbell rang. Their dinner was being delivered. They got up and ate their meals.

As they finished eating, He went after her as she ran towards the master bedroom and fell on the bed.

She said steamily: "Darling, please be easy on your Lady seeing that I just finished eating!"

He laughed and said impurely: "Ok my love! But, it will still be extreme with a gentle twist!"

She laughed as he pulled off her pajamas and, at the same time took off his own pajamas.

Then, he started kissing her all over her body as she responded to his kissing and touches.

He, then, pulled the bed sheet cover away from her and made her bend over the pillows with her belly and face lying on the bed. He raised her buttocks up and parted her legs. He penetrated her from behind as she squealed loudly with raging pleasure. He continued pounding hard into her in a recurrent rhythm for over twenty minutes. Lady Selsdon's pleasure reached an intoxicating and orgasmic climax that both of her legs became weak as both climaxed together.

He pulled out of her and both of them fell on the bed and lay down for a moment. She, then, tried to get up off the bed to use the bathroom. But, as she started walking towards the bathroom, her legs were feeble and wobbly as she staggered like a drunk with pure pleasure to the bathroom. She came back to the bedroom and laid down with her body still shaking with rhythmic pleasure. She, then, moved close to Lord Astor and laid on his chest.

They went to bed at about 11.00pm and slept the whole night.

They got up at about 8.30am and made love again. Then, they ordered breakfast at about 9.30am. Later in the day, they made love again and ate late lunch. They ordered dinner and ate their meals. At about 9.00pm, they started making love again. Lady Selsdon had great pleasure with Lord Astor that all her body responds to his touch as if she was hypnotized with wantonness!

After that lovemaking at about 10.30pm, she said lovingly: "Darling, you are making me a sex monster! That is extremely dangerous! My body cannot stop craving for you!"

He laughed and said affectionately: "It is a good thing! My whole body craves you too! I cannot stay away from you!"

She smiled weakly and said alarmingly: "But, that is dangerous! What happens if you travel for business, and I am left alone! Then, I will be burning uncontrollably when you are not here!"

He smiled and responded encouragingly, and said: "Do not worry my dear. You will be fine!"

She responded and said irresolutely: "I hope so darling! But, it is wise that we make love only on weekends so that my body will adjust to not craving for your touches till every weekend!"

He said encouragingly: "Ok dear. I will not promise to stay on that schedule!"

They went to sleep at about 11.30pm and woke at 7.30am on Monday morning. They took showers together, got dressed and he drove her to her apartment so that she can get ready for her office.

It was Tuesday evening at 9.0pm and Lady Selsdon decided to call her friends on a five-way conference line to remind them of their meeting on Friday at 11.00am to pick up their garments at the gallery.

Lady Selsdon said effervescently: "Good evening my lovely Ladies! It is getting close to my D-day!"

Lady Andrews said ebulliently: "Good evening my elegant Lady! Yes, we are all happy and getting ready. You see that I am excited because my boyfriend did stay in town after your engagement!"

Lady Ashton said naughtily: "We see that you are happy Lady Andrews! That is a strong indication that you were being fucked every day for the past three days!"

They all hollered and laughed!

Lady Ashton continued and said: "Good evening Lady Selsdon! Sorry for the interruption."

Lady Selsdon said warmly: "Thank you Lady Ashton! I was calling to inform you of two tasks that we have to accomplish this week. Firstly, we all have to stop at the gallery at 11.00am on Friday to collect our garments and ensure that it fit well with our bodies! We have to be looking good and elegant!"

Lady Bhatia said jokingly: "I know mine will fit well because I have the best shape and body relatively to you all!"

The Ladies busted out laughing because they all know that they all have fine bodies, and Lady Selsdon definitely have the best body shape of all the ladies!

Lady Adetutu added mockingly and said: "Ladies, your bodies are terrible! You all just hide behind your fine clothes! I bet your men are scared stiff to see you all naked!"

All the Ladies busted out laughing irrepressibly!

Lady Ashton said impudently: "Speak for yourself, Lady Adetutu! I know what I see in the mirror and my body is fine!"

All the Ladies started laughing again!

Lady Selsdon said: "Ladies, please let me deliver the next task. On Saturday, at about 11.00am, we all need to meet at the Dartmouth House with the team from the Bridal Group, Inc., and Lord Astor and his friends. We will have a small practice session and examine the venue, and make corrections if needed."

Lady Adetutu said supportively: "It is noted my Lady. We will be there!"

Lady Selsdon said gratefully: "Thank you Ladies and good night!"

Lady Andrews interjected and said excitedly: "Wait up Ladies! I have fantastic news to share!"

Lady Ashton said spicily: "What now Lady Andrews? That you want to invite us to a fucking orgy? The answer is 'No'!"

All the Ladies hollered and started laughing uncontrollably!

Lady Andrews said indignantly: "No, Lady Ashton. I want to announce to you all that my boyfriend proposed to me today at lunch!"

The Ladies fell silent. Then, busted out shouting 'Congratulations!' and wishing her happiness!

Lady Adetutu took a dig at her and said impertinently: "How did you achieve that feat? Did you pay him? Or, did you castrate him?"

All the ladies started shouting, laughing and continuously hollering!

Lady Selsdon said reassuringly: "Lady Andrews, we are pleased for you. We will be there to support you. Let us know when you pick a date."

Lady Andrews responded and said gratefully: "Thank you Elizabeth. I will keep you all inform!"

Then, they said their 'Good byes' and hung up the phone.

At about the same time on Tuesday, Lord Astor called his friends to inform them of the two tasks ahead for this week. They picked up the phone.

Lord Astor said warmly: "How are my gentle Lords doing this evening?"

Lord Alton said amiably: "I believe we are all well! What is up?"

Lord Astor continued and said: "We have two tasks to be completed this week and that is the reason I called."

Lord Anderson said sincerely: "What is it my Lord? Get to the point!"

Lord Astor said cordially: "Firstly, everyone should come to the gallery at 11.00am on Friday to collect their garments and ensure that it is well-fitted. As fine gentlemen, I need you all to look debonair and fine!"

Lord Ahmad said supportively: "I can guarantee you that the garments will fit us perfectly. And, do not worry, we will be looking very debonair!"

Lord Astor said jokingly: "Ok, I am rest assured that you all will be looking good!"

Lord Adeniyi interrupted said elatedly: "I have great news to share with you guys!"

Lord Alton said politely: "Can you wait till Lord Astor finish delivering his information."

Lord Astor said gratefully: "Thank you Lord Alton."

Lord Astor continued and said: "On Saturday, at about 11.00am, we all have to meet at the Dartmouth House with the Bridal Group, Inc. people, and Lady Selsdon and her friends. There is going to be a small practice session and the survey of the venue, and to ensure that all intended placements will meet with our requirements."

Lord Ahmad said: "We have this, my Lord. Do not be perturbed. We will be there!"

Lord Astor said warmly: "Lord Adeniyi, what do you have for us?"

Lord Adeniyi said effervescently: "Lady Adetutu and I are falling in love. I had discussions with her to see if she is willing to marry me. She replied affirmatively.

Therefore, I intend to propose to her next Saturday. I will let you fellows know what she say!"

Lord Astor and the other friends gave him their congratulations.

Then, Lord Anderson added excitedly: "I have formerly proposed to my girlfriend, Lady Sutton, this past weekend and she has accepted!"

All the friends started clamoring and laughing!

Lord Alton said elatedly: "It started with Lord Astor, then, followed by Lord Adeniyi, and now Lord Anderson! You all are being stolen by these elegant Ladies! There is hope for me!"

All the friends started laughing frenziedly!

Lord Astor said tenderly: "Yes, Lord Alton, there is hope for you! I know you will find love very soon!"

Lord Ahmad added jokingly: "I have greater hope because I already have a girlfriend that I intend to marry. All I need to do is summon the courage to propose!"

All the friends started laughing again!

Lord Astor said tenderly: "We will support you Lord Ahmad and give you the courage to propose!"

They all continued laughing and said 'Good night' as they hung up the phone.

At about 10.00pm, Lady Chelsea called Lord Astor in a surprise phone call.

He picked up the phone and said unexpectedly: Good evening Lady Chelsea! To what honor should I acknowledge this call?"

Lady Chelsea ignored his comment and said disappointingly: "Good evening Lord Astor! You did not even bother to check on me to see how I was fairing?"

He responded and said comfortingly: "My apologies, my Lady! The last time we met, it was not under a conducive atmosphere. I opened up a wound in your heart which I could not heal. And, if I continued calling you, the wound may get deeper! Therefore, I thought it best to give you time to heal!"

She responded and said discontentedly: "But, my Lord, the wound will not heal quickly unless you have been treating it with good words. I know you are good with words, but it will have been good if you have taken time to check on me!"

He responded and said soothingly: "My Lady, I am really sorry. It was not my intention to hurt you. I wish things were different between us. You are a good Lady and I am sure that you will find someone that will love you the way you want to be loved!"

She continued morosely: "My heart still bleeds my Lord! I will like to see you!"

He said gratifyingly and firmly: "It will not be wise for me to see you. It will open more wounds. Besides, I am already engaged and seeing you will only create more problems for both of us!"

She said sadly: "I know. I saw the announcement of your engagement and wedding in all the papers, including the Times! I thought I could see you one more time before your marriage!"

He responded and said wisely: "No, my Lady. We will get a chance to meet in the future in the gathering of friends. Please take good care of yourself and good night!"

She said forlornly: "Good night Lord Astor!"

They hung up the phone and Lord Astor went to sleep.

It was Friday morning at about 11.00am and Lord Alton, Lord Anderson and her girlfriend, Lord Ahmad and his betrothed, Lord Adeniyi and Lady Adetutu, Lady Andrews and her fiancée, Lady Ashton, Lady Bhatia and her fiancée were all seen entering the gallery. At the same time, Lord Astor was seen with Lady Selsdon as they entered the gallery hand-in-hand.

Kyle Walker welcomed them to the gallery and gave them seats so that they can be comfortable. He told them to all proceed to the dressing rooms and see if their garments fit properly.

Twenty minutes later, all the friends came back to their seats with their garments in their hands.

Lord Astor said warmly: "Thank you all my friends. Lady Selsdon and I, appreciate the time you all took from your jobs to help make our wedding a success!"

Lord Adeniyi said tenderly: "We all are happy for you! It is not a problem to take off our jobs and be with two very good humans!"

Lady Selsdon said appreciatively: "Thank you my Lord. When you all are ready to wed, we will be there also for you guys!"

Lady Bhatia said elatedly: "The wedding is two weeks from tomorrow, Saturday! We are all ready to party like rock stars!"

The friends laughed out loud as there was gaiety in the air!

Lady Andrews said excitedly: "Lord Astor, it is not a problem because we are coming to have great fun and party like no tomorrow!"

Everyone laughed again and exchanged pleasantries.

Lord Astor said informationally: "Please remember to be at Dartmouth house tomorrow at 11.00am. For those of you that have never been there, please note that the address is: 37 Charles Street, Southwest of Berkeley Square, Mayfair. See you all tomorrow."

They all assured him that they will be there as they left the gallery. Lord Astor and Lady Selsdon stayed back to conclude more arrangement with the Bridal Group, Inc.

Lord Astor said inquiringly: "Kyle, have you been to Dartmouth house to meet with the managers so that the venue can be prepared in advance?"

Kyle Walker responded and said affirmatively: "Yes, we have met with the managers. The issue is that a lot of people use Dartmouth House and we do not have enough days to prepare the venue to the level of splendor we will like to present!"

Lord Astor said firmly: "That should not be a problem. I paid for and reserved Friday and Saturday so that you can use the whole of Friday to make the venue splendid. Is one day not enough to prepare the venue?"

Kyle Walker replied and said pleasingly: "Of course, one day is enough! We will do the utmost best to ensure that the venue is magical! You will love it. I assure you!"

Lord Astor said: "Ok. We will see you tomorrow at Dartmouth House at 11.00am."

Kyle Walker said: "We will be there. Thank you."

Lord Astor and Lady Selsdon left the gallery together at about 1.00pm. Lady Selsdon called her mother and told her that she will not be coming home tonight, but, will see her and other family members tomorrow at 11.00am at Dartmouth house. She, then, told her chauffeur to take the Bentley home and that she will ride with Lord Astor.

Lord Astor and Lady Selsdon got into his navy blue Aston Martin and drove to Lady Selsdon's apartment at Kensington Place so that she can pick her night bag containing clothing items. Then, they drove to 45 Park Lane Hotel and went up to his private suite.

Immediately they entered the penthouse, Lady Selsdon jumped on Lord Astor due to her debauched and racy longing that she has suppressed for a week. He quickly closed the door behind them as she kissed Lady Selsdon passionately. She undressed him as they moved to the master bedroom. Then, she got undressed and pushed him onto the bed. She sat on him as he thrust upwards and penetrated her immediately. She kept riding him as they made love for about thirty minutes. Then, he pulled out of her and made her lay on her side as he entered her again from the side and kept thrusting into her rhythmically.

Then, he pulled out of her and got off her. She appraised his manhood and wicked cravings exploded in her body again as she became extremely wet all over again. She saw that his manhood was once more rigid, big and throbbing. She pulled him towards her so that he can enter her once more. He moved close to her and pulled her thighs apart and thrusted into her. She wailed loudly as she felt him penetrating her sturdily. He increased the speed of his thrust as she continued raising her hips in enjoyment to absorb the power of the force behind the penetration. They started making loud sounds as the gratification of their love making thrilled their bodies as they began shaking with riveting pleasure.

They kept making love together for over one hour until they were depleted and drained. He pulled out of her and held her in his hands. Then, they fell asleep.

They woke up three hours later and looked at the time. It was about 6.00pm. He decided to order room service for dinner. They got up from the bed and took showers. Then, they put on their pajamas and went to the living room to wait for their meals to be delivered.

Lady Selsdon said seductively: "I told you that you are turning me into a nymphomaniac! I am becoming a man eater! Be very careful, because I now have the capacity to devour you!"

He laughed and said lusciously: "Good! I want you to become a man eater! I want you to devour me and completely take control of me!"

She laughed and said wantonly: "I bet you like that! That, way I will become your lap dog!"

He continued laughing and said wildly: "Yes, my Lady. I like it a bunch! Then, I can worry you every night!"

She laughed and said licentiously: "So that you can be extreme with me, every night my Lord? Seriously? I decline!"

He laughed and said jestingly: "Yes. Please do not decline! I will cuddle you every night and make sure that you holler every night!"

She giggled and said playfully: "Yes, darling! Cuddling every night is what I will subscribe to! But, hollering every night sounds painful and I respectfully decline, my Lord!"

He busted out laughing and said lewdly: "Mrs. Cuddle, may I suggest that you were just hollering a moment ago and you were having a jolly good time! It was not painful, but pleasurable!"

She laughed out loud and threw one of the cushions at him. Then said cravingly: "My darling, please make your way here and cuddle me more and make me holler!"

He was so excited that he got up and went close to her and started cuddling and kissing her. Then, he tried to take her pajamas off as was giggling playfully. Then, they were interrupted!

The doorbell rang and he had to go to the door to open it so that their dinner could be delivered. They got up and ate their meals.

They finished eating their meals and she came close him and lay on his laps as they watch news and features movies on cable television.

Then, at about 9.30pm, he started cuddling and kissing her again. She got up from him and ran towards the master bedroom as he chased after her. She fell on the bed and he came close to her and pulled off her pajamas, and quickly pulled off his own pajamas. She lay naked on the bed and, he was naked standing up. Then, he looked at her naked body with wanton and decadent craving!

She said cravingly: "My love, please cuddle me gently and make me holler pleasurably so that I can live another day!"

He laughed out loud and said wickedly: "Ok darling! I will cuddle you and be extreme simultaneously so that you can live another day!"

She laughed as he got on the bed astride her. He pulled her legs apart and entered her gently as she moaned passionately.

Then, he pulled out of her and made her bend over on the bed with her tummy and face lying on the bed. He raised her buttocks up and parted her legs. He entered her from behind as she wailed loudly with uninhibited pleasure. He continued pounding hard into her in a recurrent rhythm for over twenty minutes. Lady Selsdon's pleasure was so intense that she reached an intoxicating and delirious orgasm as both of her legs became weak. Then, they both climaxed together!

He pulled out of her and both of them lay down side by side. They fell asleep and slept the whole night.

They got up at about 8.00am and ordered breakfast. Then, they took quick showers and got dressed. They ate their meals and left for their meeting with the Bridal Group, Inc. at Dartmouth House.

At about 11.00am, Lord Astor and Lady Selsdon walked into the lobby of the Dartmouth House and saw that their family members and friends were already waiting for them. They all exchanged greetings and proceeded to meet with Kyle Walker and his team.

The whole group met with the Manager of the Dartmouth House and started examining the facilities available and the architectural layout of the venue. Kyle's team was making drawings on how to place tables, chairs, flowers, ornaments, altar, live bands, food stands, beverages' stands, and other arrangements.

Then, they made a practice run on how the procession will take place. Kyle reminded everyone that they have to be back at 4.00pm on Friday, which is a day before the wedding, for final practice.

At about 2.00pm, everyone started exiting Dartmouth House. Lady Selsdon informed her parents that she will be back home to their place before 10.00am on Sunday so that she can attend church with them. Then, she left with Lord Astor as they both drove to 45 Park Lane Hotel.

Chapter 14:

The Wedding in London

Lord Astor and Lady Selsdon went upstairs to his penthouse and closed the door behind them as they got into the suite. It was about 3.30pm on the same Saturday after leaving the Dartmouth House. Lady Selsdon had untamed desire and lust in her eyes and was looking at Lord Astor with craving and longing. He, too, was looking at Lady Selsdon with wanton and obscene desire. They both took off their clothes and went into the master bedroom as raging cravings and uncontrolled hormones ran through Lady Selsdon's body. She immediately became extremely wet as she saw his erect and throbbing manhood. He pulled her legs apart and entered her as she moaned in ecstasy. They made love for over forty minutes before they reached an intoxicating and orgasmic climax.

Then, they fell asleep for over two hours and woke up around 6.30pm. He immediately ordered dinner for them, and both of them went to the bathroom to take showers together. They got out of the showers and put on their pajamas as they head towards the living room to await the delivery of their meals

Lord Astor said teasingly: "Seeing that I have been extreme with you continuously, I hope you are holding up? Are you feeling okay, my love?"

Lady Selsdon laughed and responded jestingly: "Hmmmmm! Are you holding up, my Lord? Because I am not complaining!"

He laughed out loud and said wickedly: "In that case, be ready for the next onslaught after I must have fed you and fatten you for the kill!"

She continued laughing and said vulgarly: "I am always ready for your onslaught! And, I am always ready for the kill! In fact, I want you to bring it on! However, what I worry, my Lord, is that I do not want you to fall out from exhaustion!"

He laughed frenziedly and said tawdrily: "Be prepared, my Lady! And be very scared because you brought it on yourself!"

She laughed uncontrollably and was about to respond when she was interrupted by the knocking on the door. Room service delivered their meals and they started eating a very sumptuous dinner.

After dinner, they bantered around as they watch movies on cable tv. At about 10.00pm, they made love again and went to sleep.

They woke up at around 7.30am and took showers. They got dressed and Lord Astor drove Lady Selsdon to her apartment at Kensington Place. She got in her red Jaguar Sports and drove to her parents' home in Belgravia so that she can go with her family to church.

It was the week before the wedding of Lady Selsdon and Lord Astor, and the newspapers and celebrity magazines were rife with news of the pending wedding. Pictures and professional careers of Lady Selsdon and Lord Astor were highlighted and splashed all over the papers.

Gossip columns dub it the wedding of the year between two billionaires!

The week was very routine for all family members and friends of Lady Selsdon and Lord Astor as gaiety and joyous atmosphere surrounded the pending couple. Lady Selsdon went to lunch with Lord Astor on Monday and Wednesday, and was looking forward to their date on Friday and the whole weekend.

After dinner on Thursday evening, at about 9.00pm, Lady Selsdon decided to touch base with her friends. She called them on a five-way conference line and they all picked up their calls.

Lady Selsdon said elatedly: "Good evening my friends! I hope you all have been enjoying yourselves as you prepare for my wedding next week!"

Lady Adetutu said enthusiastically: "Yes, Elizabeth! We are getting ready and we are very happy for you!"

Lady Selsdon said: "Thank you Lady Adetutu!"

Lady Bhatia said cautiously: "Good evening Lady Selsdon! We are ready to dance the night away at your wedding! But, are you ready to be a wife?"

Everyone was quiet and did not like the tone of Lady Bhatia as they feel that the question was inappropriate!

Lady Selsdon responded and said inquiringly: "What do you mean Lady Bhatia?"

Lady Bhatia replied and said factually: "You know after the fun of the wedding, then, you have to do wifely things, have children, keep home, cook your husband's favorite food, and go to work! All at the same time! Are you prepared for it?"

All the friends busted out laughing and told Lady Bhatia to 'Hush'!!

Lady Andrews answered and said forbiddingly: "Lady Bhatia, please hush up! What else will Lady Selsdon do, but get fucked every day! That is the duty of the wife! She is already doing it and you can tell she loves it with the sudden glow all over her face! So, she is definitely well prepared to be a wife!"

All the friends hollered, laughed hysterically, and kept clapping!

Lady Ashton said friskily: "Hush up Lady Andrews! In your sexual perverted mind, you think being fucked every day is all that a wife does? Wow! What planet are you from?"

Everyone hollered, laughed side-splittingly, and kept clapping!

Lady Selsdon responded to both Ladies and said tenderly: "Lady Bhatia and Lady Andrews, I am fully prepared to be a wife! I can cook. I am not lazy. I do work. I have not discussed with my husband-to-be on how many children he wants. However, we will reach a compromise on that. But, most significantly is the fact that I love him and he loves me! And with love, it will be a pleasure to do his biddings! So, yes I am very ready to be a wife!"

All the friends hollered, laughed uproariously, and kept clapping, and saying 'Well said, Elizabeth'!

Lady Selsdon continued and said fondly: "So, my Ladies, please be prepared to come the following Friday at 3.00pm for rehearsal and my wedding for the day after!"

All the friends laughed elatedly and assured her that they will be there!

Then, Lady Andrews interjected and said happily: "We have chosen our own wedding date! It will be the last Saturday of August! And, you all will be there to support me!"

Everyone cheered, hollered, laughed hilariously, and kept clapping!

Lady Selsdon said happily: "Congratulations Lady Andrews! We will definitely be there to support you!"

Lady Adetutu said excitedly: "Congratulations my Lady! You deserve to be happy and we will be there for you!"

Lady Bhatia mimicked the prevailing sentiments and said enthusiastically: "Congratulations Lady Andrews! I hope you are really, really, really prepared to be a wife?"

All the friends again, bawled, laughed riotously, and kept clapping!

Then, Lady Ashton added blissfully: "Lady Andrews, congratulations and we are pleased for you! However, in support of Lady Bhatia, I advise you to go quickly learn other wifely skills instead of focusing on fucking!"

Everyone bellowed, laughed uproariously, and kept clapping!

Then, Lady Adetutu added elatedly and said surprisingly: "I am engaged! I am engaged! I am engaged! Thank you Lady Selsdon for the connection! I am in love! Lord Adeniyi proposed to me last week and I accepted! We have already agreed to be married on the last Saturday in September!"

Everyone applauded again, shrieked, laughed uproariously, and kept clapping!

Lady Selsdon said happily: "All these are good news everywhere! Congratulations Lady Adetutu! And, you are welcome! For sure, we will definitely be there to support you!"

Lady Adetutu said excitedly: "Thank you!"

Lady Bhatia said happily: "Congratulations Lady Adetutu! I know that you are really prepared to be a wife!"

Lady Adetutu said hilariously: "Yes! For sure! I am prepared!"

All the friends again, howled, laughed wildly, and kept clapping!

Then, Lady Ashton added joyfully: "Lady Adetutu, congratulations my friend and I am exceedingly pleased for you!"

And, then, Lady Andrews while addressing Lady Adetutu, added and said indecently: "That means you have allowed Lord Adeniyi to be fucking you every day and you just met him less than three weeks ago! You must be enjoying it tremendously for you to have accepted to marry him that quickly!"

Lady Adetutu replied and said vulgarly: "Yes! He has been fucking me every day and I am enjoying it tremendously better than what you are enjoying!"

Everyone hollered, laughed raucously, and kept clapping!

They continued to banter till about 10.30pm before they hung up and went to bed.

At about the same time, around 9.00pm on the same Thursday, Lord Astor decided to reach out to his friends. He called them on a five-way conference call and they all picked up their phones.

Lord Astor said animatedly: "Good evening my fine gentlemen! Hope all is well with the finest English Lords in Britain!"

Lord Alton responded and said jokingly: "Good evening Lloyd! What is with the sycophancy?"

Lord Astor said eagerly: "I am just happy my Lord! My wedding is a week away and I cannot wait to have Lady Selsdon moved into my place!"

Lord Adeniyi said fervently: "Good evening my Lord! We get it! We are happy for you! What else do you need?"

Lord Astor responded and said warmly: "Thank you! Please do not forget that everyone has to be at the rehearsals at 3.00pm the following Friday and be ready for the wedding the next day!"

Lord Ahmad said amiably: "Lloyd, I can see that you are really excited! We will be there. Do not worry! We have your back! The only issue is that you will not be at our next Polo match because you will be too busy on your honeymoon!"

Everyone hailed, howled, laughed hilariously, and kept clamoring!

Lord Astor said: "Thank you Lord Ahmad! I will join you in the next Polo match after the one that I will miss! That is, if I have enough energy left after my honeymoon to play a game!"

All the friends continued bawling, howling, laughing uproariously, and kept clamoring!

Then, Lord Anderson said enthusiastically: "The wedding date for Lady Sutton and I have been set for the third Saturday of August! I hope Lord Astor will be back from his honeymoon and you guys will be around to support me!"

Lord Astor said assuredly: "Congratulations my Lord! I will be back! Rest assured. We will be there to support you!"

Lord Alton said assuredly: "We all will be in town to support you. Congratulations!"

Lord Ahmad said lively: "Great job, my Lord! We will be ready to get down!"

Lord Adeniyi said buoyantly: "Lord Anderson, you are good fella and Lady Sutton must be very happy to have found love in your hands!"

Then, Lord Adeniyi continued and said startlingly: "I am engaged also to Lady Adetutu! I proposed last week and she accepted! Thanks to Lord Astor and Lady Selsdon for connecting us! They helped me found my love! We have set a date to be wed on the last Saturday of September!"

Lord Astor said in a congratulatory tone: "Awesome, my Lord! Congratulations! Lady Selsdon and I will definitely be there to support you!"

Lord Anderson said elatedly: "Congratulations my Lord! It is happening to all of us! We are being taken off the list of eligible bachelors in London!"

Lord Ahmad mirrored the prevalent sentiments and said heartily: "Congratulations Lord Adeniyi! Your bride to be will have a jolly good time and give you a lot of 'toto' and a lot of children!"

All the friends again, howled, laughed side-splittingly, and kept clapping!

Lord Alton, then, added and said delightfully: "I am happy for you Lord Adeniyi! We will all be there to party down at your wedding! It is going to be a busy summer! But, I have not been spoken for! I need to up my game and find me a gorgeous Lady that I can fall in love with! Any pointers from you fellows?"

Everyone bellowed, laughed uproariously, and kept clapping!

Lord Astor responded and said encouragingly: "Lord Alton, relax. We will find you the finest lady in London that will truly appreciate you! Do not worry!"

They continued to banter for few more minutes before they retired for bed.

At about 10.00pm, Lord Astor made a call to Lady Selsdon and she picked up the phone. She can hear the excitement in his voice.

Lord Astor said lovingly: "Good evening, darling! I hope I did not wake you up?"

Lady Selsdon said alluringly: "No my dear. But, I am already in bed. What is in your mind?"

He replied and said warmly: "Just checking on your comfort my love!"

She responded and said adoringly: "That is sweet my Lord! I am good. What time are you picking me up tomorrow for our weekend date?

He answered said lively: "Early! Can we do 2.00pm?"

She responded and said seductively: "2.00pm is good for me! You know I cannot wait to see you and be in your hands! I am already missing you!"

He responded teasingly and said beguilingly: "Seriously, darling! You know I have been missing you the whole week! I can't wait to see you tomorrow!"

She laughed and said warmly: "Good night my, love!"

He responded and said tenderly: "Good night, darling!"

They hung up and went to sleep.

At about 1.00pm on a Friday afternoon, Lady Selsdon arrived at her apartment at Kensington Place so that she can get prepared for her date with Lord Astor. She called and notified her parents that she will be with Lord Astor and will not be seeing them on Sunday till Monday afternoon.

She decided to pack extra clothing and underwear in her night bag. She took a bath and dressed in a flowery navy blue dress which highlighted her blue eyes! She looked in the mirror and said to herself haughtily: "Lord Astor, you brought it on yourself, man! I am going to be extreme and wear you down tonight! I am the hottest I have ever been, even fierier than a volcano! It is a week away before I officially become your wife! I look beautiful! Bring it on my fine gentleman!"

Underneath her dress, she had a navy blue bra and under pant plus a navy blue slip. She put on her seven-carat diamond ring and some wicked perfume. Then, she decided that she was ready for a very naughty rendezvous with her betrothed! At about 2.00pm, the door to her apartment buzzed. She opened the door and Lord Astor stood there smiling. She thought: "My goodness! Lloyd you are a dangerous and fine man! A hunk of a real gentleman!" She was suddenly very wet and hoped to be laid by him right there!

She took her mind of the gutter and, said feebly and playfully: "My love, you looked damn fine! Where are we going?"

He laughed and said jokingly: "You look damn stunning yourself, darling! The occasion is a dangerous liaison with my wife! What are your enthralling thoughts this evening, my Lady?"

She giggled and said: "A very dangerous rendezvous, indeed! Hmmm! My Lord, you should be much scarred of your Lady because I have very dangerous and sinister thoughts that have your name all wrapped in it!"

He laughed more and said rascally: "Seriously! Are you suggesting that I should be scarred, madam! What types of wicked thoughts do you have in mind, my Lady?"

Lady Selsdon said seductively: "You will see! I feel sorry for you! Shall we go now to our dangerous rendezvous?"

He laughed out loud and said brazenly: "Please have mercy on me, my Lady!"

They both laughed as they exited her apartment.

They got in Lord Astor's navy blue Aston Martin and drove towards 45 Park Lane Hotel. He parked and they went upstairs as they took the elevator to the penthouse suite. He opened the door and they went into the luxurious suite.

She walked into the master bedroom and placed her night bag in the closet and said: "Darling, I am hungry!"

He said: "Yep! I famished too. Are we eating in or going downstairs?"

She said audaciously: "Did you think I put on this elegant dress for you so that you can easily tear it off me? Seriously! Pardon my haughtiness! But, I want to be seen in your hand as usual and to show off my diamond! Call me shameless! Let's go downstairs and eat so that I can be seen by people with my husband!"

He laughed out loud and tried to kiss her, but she ran away and said: "Not now, darling! You will mess up my make-up!"

He kept laughing and said: "Ok! Let's go eat!"

They went downstairs and were taken to a private section of the restaurant. They decided to eat a seafood meal plus drink white wine.

Lord Astor said delightfully: "I am excited that our house is ready! We will be meeting the designer on Monday afternoon so that you can tell her how you want the house designed and what types of furniture you want.

This way, it will be ready when we get back from our honeymoon!"

Lady Selsdon said delightfully: "Ok! It sounds exciting! But, you know that after Monday, I will not be available to see you till Friday for rehearsals and Saturday for the wedding!"

He laughed and said: "Ok, my dear! That is a small sacrifice to make for a Lady I will be spending the rest of my life with!"

She giggled and said playfully: "Thank you my love for your understanding! Where are we going for our honeymoon?"

He laughed and replied enthusiastically: "I wanted a very private place for our honeymoon! Where we will not be disturbed! Like a private island in Bali! Is that good for you my very fearless Lady?"

She laughed too and said playfully: "Bali sounds enchanting and falls into one of those very dangerous rendezvous! Do you think I should be scared because you will have too much liberty to be extreme with, and no one to shout to for help?"

He busted out laughing in frenzy and said teasingly: "My darling, I have told you before that you have extremely dangerous wits! You are right! You should be scarred because there will be no one for you to call for help! I intend to make love to you every day and ensure that it is very extreme!"

She continued to giggle for a while and said playfully: "Wow! Seriously! Lloyd, you are going to be merciless with your wife! Not good qualities for a fine English gentleman! I will have to report you to the queen for all your intended follies! Albeit, I may just disappoint you and thoroughly enjoy your dangerous and extreme follies!"

He laughed irrepressibly loud as some of the diners looked towards their table to see them enjoying themselves! He responded and said jokingly: "My follies, my dear, will be to your extreme pleasure! I can assure you, darling! You make me laugh so much my love!"

Then, their food was served and they started eating.

As she did earlier on in their relationship, Lady Selsdon again placed one of her legs on the lap of Lord Astor under the table where no one can see what she was doing! He pulled the leg more to his lap and tickled her toes. She giggled out loud and some diners looked towards their table again!

He smiled and said mischievously: "My Lady, you are outrageous! Is it one of your follies to make love to me here in public?"

She giggled more and said depravedly: "Why not? Are you scarred? I see you are ready! Because I can feel your erection here under the table in public!"

He laughed out loud in frenzy as he was enjoying the moment with her bride-to-be! He said spicily: "What I have turned you into? A promiscuous English Lady that cannot control her passion in public! Should I report to the Queen, or should I be very scarred, my Lady?

Lady Selsdon started laughing hysterically and said innocently: "Seriously! My Lord, please do not put the denunciation on me because you could not handle the heat which you brought on yourself! I think you should be really scarred of me and my sinister thoughts!"

Lord Astor continued to laugh wildly and said naughtily: "My Lady, I intend to make you beg for mercy under extreme circumstances!"

Still laughing, she said delightfully: "Lloyd, I can't wait for you to make me beg for mercy!" Nonetheless, seeing that I love you a bunch, I will show mercy on you!"

He said romantically: "Elizabeth, I love you a bunch my darling!"

She laughed and inquired seriously: "We have not discussed one more thing. How many children do you want me to bear for you?"

Lord Astor replied and said lovingly: "How about seven!"

She laughed out loud and said saucily: "Seriously! What am I? A rabbit?"

He laughed out loud too and said playfully: "Do not be perturbed my Lady! I was only joking! On a serious note, how about three?"

She smiled and said agreeably: "Three is logical! Can we wait for two years and let me enjoy you for a while before we start thinking of and planning for children?"

He smiled and mimicked her, and said agreeable: "That is logical too!"

They finished eating their meals at about 4.30pm and decided to go upstairs. She put her leg down and got up as he came around and kissed her ardently. Then, they walked out together as she put her hand into his elbow. They rode the elevator up as he held her close to himself

As they got into the penthouse suite, he closed the door and kissed her overpoweringly and carried her to the master bedroom. He started by taking off his own clothes. Then, he gently, started taking off all her clothes including her bra and underpants. She lay naked looking extremely gorgeous, and looking up at him in a delirious manner with sinful desires!

Lord Astor looked at the naked body of Elizabeth and wicked cravings shut through his body as he became erect with an enormous manhood! She saw his erection and she became extremely wet with inebriating desire. He pushed her legs open and entered her powerfully. She shouted in ecstatic pleasure and whimper as he kept thrusting into her in rapid manner. She kept squirming under him as he kept pounding away into her. Her body was shaking in rhythmic pleasure as she was enjoying his forceful thrust. He was extremely enjoying his bride-to-be as he kept the pace going on for over forty minutes! He pulled out of her and turned her around and entered her from the back. He started pounding her from behind forcefully and kept plunging speedily into her as she was having orgasmic pleasure. After another twenty minutes of love making, they both reached an earth-shattering and mind-altering climax!

He pulled out of her and drew her close to himself. They were drained and smashed as if drunk with hard liquor!

As Lady Selsdon laid in his hands, she thought to herself that she was always having hypnotic sexual pleasure with him! She thoroughly relishes their lovemaking! She said lasciviously: "My Lord, that was extreme and intense! You are turning me into a wanton sexual pervert! I should be very scarred!"

He was having the same mirrored thought because he has never enjoyed any woman like he does Elizabeth! He relishes thoroughly their love making and concluded that it was the best sexual experience he ever had! He laughed and said licentiously: "You said you were not scared! Then, you brought it on yourself, my love! I gave you extreme as per your request, madam!"

She started laughing and said enticingly and mischievously: "Please my Lord, have mercy on your frightened subject!"

He started laughing frenziedly: "Ok, my dear! You shall receive mercy only if you tell me that you love me, extremely!"

She laughed and said: "Darling, I love you, extremely!"

They laughed and conversed playfully into the night. At about 8.00pm, they ate dinner. Then, two hours later, they made love again and fell asleep as they rested throughout the whole night.

They got up late in the morning at about 9.00am on Saturday. Then, he made love to her again for over thirty minutes. At about 9.30am, they got up and took showers together.

As they got out of the shower, he attempted to make love to her again, but she ran away from him and said friskily: "Not now my love! I am famished! Remember that you promised to feed me and fatten me for the kill! Where is my breakfast?"

He kept laughing and said temptingly: "Do you know what you are missing, Elizabeth? More extreme pleasure!"

She was laughing too and said lovingly: "I know my, my dear! But not now! Please order room service so that I can have a good breakfast."

He said lovingly: "Okay, darling!"

He, then, ordered room service while they watched the news on tv as they wait for their meals. About twenty minutes later, their breakfast was brought up and laid out in the living room.

They ate and rested for a while. Then, he made love to her again for another forty minutes. They fell asleep and woke up at about 3.00pm. They forewent lunch and opted for early dinner. They conversed and played till 6.00 pm before ordering early dinner. Two hours later, they made love for over two hours as they explored various sex positions in their crave to pleasure themselves. They fell asleep and slept the whole night.

On Sunday, they repeated the same routine they had the previous day. By Sunday night, their bodies were tired from all their marathon sex acts. They slept the whole night and woke up at about 8.0am.

It was Monday morning and Lady Selsdon declined any lovemaking and had him take her to her apartment to get ready for office. She went to her office briefly and, then, dashed to meet Lord Astor and the designer at their new house in Belgravia. Once she got there, she discussed choice of colors, types of furniture, and other decorations needed for the new house. They finished discussions at about 4.00pm, and Lady Selsdon left for her parents' home as Lord Astor went to One Grosvenor Square.

It was the week of the wedding! And, there was excitement and gaiety in the air in both the Selsdon's home and the Astor's home. Preparations were being made, and families and friends were constantly calling. It was a joyful and idyllic week full of sweet anticipation of good times to be enjoyed!

It was Friday afternoon at about 3.00pm. Kyle Walter, David Bradley, Joan Robert, and Barbara Smith including members of their staff were already inside the hall at Dartmouth House. Actually, they have been there since 7.00am with enormous amount of equipment, decorations, flowers, tables, chairs, altar, stands for live band, food and beverages, and beautiful ornaments!

They were putting finishing touches to the design and construction of the inside main hall for the wedding. It was magical! It was splendid! There was beauty everywhere! It looked fairy-tale-like and it was enough to enchant anyone to want to get married!

There were twenty-five designed areas for the guests with each area having subtle, but vibrant colors. One of the designed areas was reserved for dancing and about twenty designed areas were reserved for guests' sittings. Each of the twenty designed areas has seats and tables for forty-five guests. Another four designed areas were reserved for live bands, buffet and drinks stand, and the marriage altar. Kyle Walter and his staff from the Bridal Group, Inc. were carefully examining every detail of the designs and structures created for the wedding event.

Baron Selsdon, Baroness Selsdon, Lady Selsdon, Olivia, and Jane arrived at about 3.00pm and walked into the main hall of Dartmouth House and they were suddenly flabbergasted at the designed areas and all the decorations. They were dumbfounded at the beauty of the design areas and the layout of other structures. It was Magical! At about the same time, Lady Selsdon's friends, twenty invited children and other members of the bridal train arrived. They were all astonished at the beauty of the decorations in the main hall. They walked down the red carpet, and there were continuous chatter and excitement as they gave accolades to the Bridal Group, Inc.

At about 3.10pm, Baron Astor, Baroness Astor, Lord Astor and his friends, and other members of the groom's train arrived at Dartmouth House. Also, the officiating priest arrived at the site simultaneously. Baron Astor and everyone in his group were astounded at the stunning design, the beautiful flowers adorning the tables and the designed areas, and the magnificent and exquisite design of other structures. The groom and his family members were happy at the fabulous designs! It was indeed magical!" The groups from the Bride and Groom started intermingling, conversing, and chattering in excitement as they gave great compliments to the Bridal Group, Inc.

At about 4.00pm, the rehearsals started. The Groom and his friends walked to the wedding alter as the bride and the bridal train walked down the long aisle on the magnificent red carpet. The twenty children walked in front of the bridal train as they spread roses on the red carpet. The wedding rehearsals were stunning and magical! It was a lens to look into and a forerunner of what the actual wedding will look like on Saturday morning! Once, all the guests are present on Saturday and the music starts playing, the wedding event will definitely come alive and be enchanting as if everyone was in a fairy-tale land! The rehearsals were successful and everyone left about 6.00pm to go home and prepare for the wedding on Saturday morning.

It was Saturday morning at about 9.00am. Kyle Walter, David Bradley, Joan Robert, and Barbara Smith were all present at the wedding venue, and were exquisitely dressed in white suits and navy blue ties. Also, the hosts and hostesses, and waiters and waitresses were dressed in white attires with navy blue ties as they ushered in various guests. Most of the guests were people that were Dukes, Duchesses, Barons, Baronesses, Lords, Ladies, Captains of Industries, and filthy rich people that were attired appropriately and reflected their wealth. The men were wearing impeccable fitting suits with navy blue hats or navy blue ties. The ladies were attired in immaculately designed dresses in all sorts of hue that has something with navy blue in it. All the guests had something that had navy blue as part of their attire – like hats, ties, sashes, and broaches. This was a big wedding with guests close to about 850 people! There were TV personalities, celebrities, captain of industries, bankers, and editors from the various magazines, including Vogue magazine, that were present. This was a high profile wedding with various celebrities from everywhere arriving for the event. Kyle, David, Joan and Barbara were moving around the guests and ensuring that they were comfortable.

There were beautiful flowers adorning the tables and around the designed areas. The drinks and buffet tent was well-loaded with all types of delicacies and all sort of wines and liquors. The live band was playing various music ranging from music by the Beatles, jazz, rhythm and blues, and salsa to pop rock. There was gaiety in the air and everything looked magical, enchanted and fairylike.

At about 10.00am, the hosts and hostesses directed the waiters and waitresses to start serving wines and other various drinks to the guests. Guests were interacting, talking and having fun.

At about 10.15am, Baroness Selsdon and some of her close friends plus some family members arrived at the location and walked down the aisle and sat down. At the same time, Baron Astor, Baroness Astor and their family members plus some close friends walked in and sat by Baroness Selsdon. They all exchanged pleasantries. They were all dressed elegantly and expensively and had some accessories that were colored in navy blue. Soon after, Baroness Selsdon and Baron Astor got up and started making small conversations with the guests and some of their friends by going around some design areas.

After a short time, Baroness Selsdon walked away from the wedding hall and headed towards the special dressing room reserved for the bride and her bridal train to ensure that her daughter was well-presented and emotionally ready for the wedding. She went into the dressing room and saw her husband, Olivia, Jane and Lady Selsdon's four friends, and the twenty little children.

Baroness Selsdon was stunned at the elegance and beauty of her daughter! She was dazzling and glowing, and she has never seen her daughter this ravishingly beautiful! Lady Selsdon's white wedding gown had a little sash colored in navy blue, and was embroidered with lace which was exquisitely crafted and designed to hug and fit her body effortlessly. Her hair was packed and fixed flawlessly. Her make-up was applied impeccably. She looked like a Hollywood goddess!

Baroness Selsdon scrutinized her daughter and said pompously and wondrously: "Elizabeth, you look astonishing and spellbindingly beautiful! This is a day I will never forget! It is a day that is specially made for you! Enjoy it, my dear!"

Everyone present in the room giggled and clapped their hands. They all echoed the same thoughts and said: "Yes, she looks like a beautiful movie star!"

Lady Selsdon looked at her mother, father and her bridal train and said courteously: "Thank you mom, dad, Olivia, and Jane! And, thank you friends. You all have been very benevolent to me in ensuring that my day was perfect and pleasant!"

Lady Selsdon's four friends, Lady Andrews, Lady Adetutu, Lady Bhatia, and Lady Ashton were exquisitely attired in designed navy blue dresses with their hair and makeup done flawlessly. The twenty children, ten boys and ten girls, were dressed richly and perfectly.

At the other special dressing room, Lord Astor and his four friends were wearing tailored and stripped grey suits with navy blue ties plus specially crafted grey hats with navy blue sash. They looked very rich like perfect English Lords. Lord Astor was looking very handsome, debonair and noble in his perfectly tailored suit. They were laughing and getting ready to walk to the stage were the altar was located.

At exactly 10.45am, Kyle Walter, the Master of Ceremony, told the live band to stop playing. He welcomed all the guests and told them that the ceremony was about to start. He announced the order of the ceremony as stated in the wedding brochure given to the guests. He ordered the bridegroom and his best man, and friends to proceed to the designed area with the altar where the priest was already standing.

The guests were looking with pleasure as the groom, Lord Astor, and his friends, Lord Adetutu, Lord Ahmad, Lord Anderson, and Lord Alton started walking to the front of the altar and stood before the priest, and smiled and nodded to the priest.

At exactly 10.55am, the Master of Ceremony ordered the live band to commence playing the bridal song as the bridal train started walking down the aisle. All the guests stood up as the bridal train approached the red carpet. The twenty children were in front and each had small navy blue buckets filled with navy blue roses' petals. As the children were walking down the aisle, they started sprinkling the petals on the red carpet so that the bride will walk on them. The bride, Lady Selsdon, was being held in the arm by his father, Baron Selsdon, and both were walking on the red carpet behind the children as they progressed towards the altar to meet the groom. Lord Selsdon's four friends were walking behind her and the dad, and were carrying navy blue bouquet of flowers.

All the guests gushed, oozed, cooed, and babbled as they saw the stunning beauty of Lady Selsdon as she walked seductively and elegantly with her characteristic gait! The men were indecently slavering and the women were being envious of her perfect beauty. A gorgeous goddess indeed!

The bridal train got to the front of the altar and Baron Selsdon let go Lady Selsdon's arm as she stood close to Lord Astor. The groom and the bride smiled to each other. Then, Baron Selsdon went and stood by his wife, Baroness Selsdon, as all the other guests remained standing. The bridesmaid stood on the left side of Lady Selsdon, while the best men stood on the right side of Lord Astor.

The Mater of Ceremony gave signal to the live band to stop the bridal song as the priest moved to stand in front of the bride and the groom. There was quiet as the priest started the ceremony.

The Priest smiled and said warmly: "Good morning ladies and gentlemen. Please, all should be seated except for the bride and her bridesmaid, and the groom and his best men."

All the guests and family members sat down.

The Priest continued: "Today, we are here present in the sight of the Lord to join Lord Astor and Lady Selsdon in Holy Matrimony. If, there is someone who says that this union should not take place, then he or she should say so now or forever remain silent."

The priest paused and surveyed the guests. There was no objection. So, he proceeded with the ceremony.

He looked at the bride and groom and said: "Each of you will repeat after me when I call upon you to do so."

The bride and groom nodded their heads.

The Priest said to Lord Astor: "Please repeat after me: 'I, Lord Astor, take thee, Lady Selsdon, to be my wedded Wife, to have and to hold from this day forward, for better for worse, for richer for poorer, in sickness and in health, to love and to cherish, till death us do part, according to God's holy ordinance; and thereto I plight thee my troth'"

Lord Astor repeated the words as he was facing Lady Selsdon.

Then, the Priest said to Lady Selsdon: "Repeat after me: 'I, Lady Selsdon, take thee, Lord Astor, to be my wedded Husband, to have and to hold from this day forward, for better for worse, for richer for poorer, in sickness and in health, to love, cherish, and to obey, till death us do part, according to God's holy ordinance; and thereto I give thee my troth'"

Lady Selsdon repeated the words as he was facing Lord Astor.

The Priest, then, told the groom to place the ring on the bride's finger, and say the following: "With this Ring I thee wed, with my body I thee worship, and with all my worldly goods I thee endow: In the name of the Father, and of the Son, and of the Holy Ghost. Amen."

Lord Astor repeated the words as he was putting the ring on the left ring finger of Lady Selsdon.

The Priest, then, told the bride to place the ring on the groom's finger, and say the following: "With this Ring I thee wed, with my body I thee worship, and with all my worldly goods I thee endow: In the name of the Father, and of the Son, and of the Holy Ghost. Amen."

Lady Selsdon repeated the words as he was putting the ring on the left ring finger of Lord Astor.

The Priest said to the couple: "I now pronounce you Husband and Wife. Lord Astor, you may now kiss your bride."

Lord Astor held Lady Selsdon and kissed her passionately. The guests and all family members stood up and applauded. Lord Astor and Lady Selsdon, and their trains walked to their seats and sat down.

The Master of Ceremony took the microphone and told the Live Band to start playing and instructed the waiters and waitresses to start serving food and drinks.

After another hour, the Master of Ceremony ordered that the waiters and waitresses to start serving champagne as Lady Ashton was getting ready to give a speech and toast the bride.

Lady Ashton said enthusiastically and jokingly: "My Lord, My Ladies, and all you elegant and gorgeous people! Thank you for taking the time to honor my best friend! This best friend of mine here, is possible the most beautiful, kindhearted and loving human on this planet!" She pointed to Lady Selsdon as the guests were looking and laughing.

She continued and said laughingly: "There are plenty fine brides in London, but only one is an actual goddess from Venus! Such a beauty! Such a fine goddess! Such a kind goddess! That is Lady Selsdon! Lord Astor should not be allowed to appropriate this goddess for himself!"

All the guests fell out laughing. She continued: "But, then, as you all know, even Venus fell in love! So, we should give Lady Selsdon liberties to fall in love with a commoner like the very handsome Lord Astor!"

There was more uncontrollable laughter by all the guests. Then, Lady Ashton continued and narrated the history of their friendship and how she and her friends played various parts in supporting the engagement of Lady Selsdon to Lord Astor.

She, then, concluded and said: "Any noble Lord will be lucky to have Lady Selsdon! She is not just a beautiful woman, but, a brilliant, kind and astute lady. Lord Astor is a lucky gentleman to have Lady Selsdon falls in love with him. I wish both of them a blessed and long life. Please, stand up and toast to Lord and Lady Astor!"

All the guests stood up and toasted to Lady and Lord Astor.

Then, Lord Alton, one of the best men stood up to toast the couple. He made jokes and gave the history of their friendship, and how the relationship between Lord Astor and Lady Selsdon developed.

Lord Alton concluded by saying: "While Lady Selsdon may be from Venus, Lord Astor is definitely from Mars because he is a warrior, assertive, and passionate. Therefore, this union is a match made in the stars and only evident to us humans because we have been waiting for its manifestation!"

Everyone laughed frenziedly and stood up and applauded.

Lord Alton said boisterously: "Please stand up and toast to my best friend and his new bride, and wish them good life!"

There were noises of guests toasting and wishing the bride and groom best wishes.

Then, the couple was called to the dance floor as they danced, and were joined by guests. The wedding was truly magical and a huge success!

At about 7.00pm, Lord Astor and Lady Selsdon started exiting the wedding hall and heading towards the Rolls Royce that will take them towards their honeymoon destination. Then, the guests started exiting the wedding hall at about 7.30pm. Everyone had a jolly good time!

Chapter 15:

The Honeymoon in Bali

It is still Saturday evening at about 7.10pm and Lord Astor and Lady Astor are seen holding hands inside the Rolls Royce that is decorated with bridal flowers. The chauffeur started driving towards London Heathrow Airport. As he was driving away, the groom and bride started surveying the scenery, the manicured gardens and parks, the elegant buildings, and high rise office buildings that line the streets of London. The chauffeur drove to a private hangar where a brand new Gulfstream G650ER Jet Aircraft was packed. Lord Astor bought it for his bride as a wedding gift! The cost was $65 million! As Lord Astor and Lady Astor got out of the Rolls Royce, and got close to the brand new Jet, they saw that the Jet was massive and majestic. The aircraft was painted in blue with "ELIZABETH" and engraved in gold on all sides of the Jet!

There was immense surprise on the face of Lady Astor!

Lady Astor was dumbfounded and, at the same time, thrilled! She looked at her husband and asked: "You bought this for me?"

Lord Astor said pleasingly to his bride: "Yes, it is for you darling! I bought this for you as a special wedding gift to show that I love you a bunch!"

Elizabeth was overjoyed and looked at her husband affectionately and hopped into his hands and said: "Thank you my love! I love you a bunch too!"

Lloyd picked up Elizabeth in his hands and kissed her passionately while carrying her up the staircase of the Aircraft. As they got into the Jet, he put her down and she saw one of the most well-appointed, magnificent and opulent spaces in a Jet that she has ever seen! The Captain and his crew welcomed them on board. Then, Lloyd and Elizabeth went to the private bedroom in the back of the aircraft to remove their wedding clothes and put on casual traveling clothes. The private bedroom had a super-sized king bed. And as they went into the bedroom, Lady Astor fell on the bed.

She said to her husband: "My love, I am exhausted! I know I need to change, but I am tired!"

Lord Astor said compassionately: "I understand, darling! You have been on your feet for over twelve hours. Do you want dinner and drinks?"

She replied wearily: "Not now. Give me a little respite and some sleep for about two hours before ordering. When are flying out?"

Lord Astor responded and said tenderly: "We should be flying out in the next one hour. So, go ahead and try to sleep. I will wake you up later. It is a long flight to Bali which is in Indonesia. We will, probably, stop to fuel in New Delhi. We should be back to London in ten days."

Elizabeth said: "Ok, husband. Please, help me and unzip my dress so that I can take off my bridal dress."

Lord Astor indulged her and softly took off her bridal dress and camisole.

He, then, said playfully: "Should I help you take off your white panties and bra?"

Elizabeth giggled and said firmly: "Not now dear! Maybe later! But, please do not take advantage of your tired bride!"

Lloyd responded and said understandingly: "Ok, sweetheart! I will pull the bed covers on you while you get some rest. In the meantime, I will go upfront to the living area and get some drinks. I will come and lay by your side in about thirty minutes and fall asleep also.

She said: "Ok." And fell asleep.

Lord Astor took of his suit and changed into casual wears, and went to the living area to get some drink while watching as the Captain and the crews prepare the aircraft to fly out of London Heathrow Airport.

At about 10.30pm, Elizabeth got up and saw her husband lying beside her. She took the hands of Lloyd and put it on her breasts. He woke up and took of her bra and started playing with her nipples. Then, he pulled off her white undergarments. He quickly pulled off his casual clothing and started kissing her all over her body. She was fully naked and looking exquisite and stunning. Lord Astor's manhood got bigger and turgid. Elizabeth looked at her husband and was still stunned at the size of his manhood. Even, after the very first time they made love she always avoided trying to focus on it. She saw that his manhood was big and long, and throbbing. He came close to her and turned her around with her buttocks facing him. He, then, put some pillows underneath her so that her buttocks will be raised up.

She said playfully: "Darling, we are in a Jet and you know I make a lot of noise. The crew will hear me making all that noise!"

He laughed and said teasingly and factually: "Do not worry my dear! You can make all the noise you want, but they will hear nothing because this room is soundproofed!"

She giggled and said playfully: "Then, you can be extreme with me!"

He laughed and said: "At your pleasure, darling! I intend to be extreme!"

Lloyd, then, made her to face the mirror so that she can see what he is about to do to her. She was extremely wet with her body shaking with desires and longing for him to enter her. He obliged her and entered her from behind as both of them watched their lovemaking in the mirror.

Elizabeth's body exploded with rapture as her whole body was on heat. She groaned loudly and shamelessly. The, she started wriggling with sheer ecstasy. She was watching everything in the mirror as he was pounding away into her. Lord Astor was having great fun with his wife as he watched himself entering in and out of her. He kept making love to her this way for over thirty-five minutes. Then, he turned her over and entered her again from the front and made love to her for over one hour till both of them climaxed. He pulled out of her and they both lay side by side completely exhausted.

They looked at the time. It was past midnight and they were already airborne flying towards Bali Island.

Elizabeth moved closer to Lloyd and laid in his hands. She said languidly: "My love, that was too extreme on a plane! That is new for me!"

He laughed and responded cleverly, and provocatively: "Do you need more extreme follies, madam?"

Elizabeth responded and inquired seductively: "Is it the type of follies that involve wild and crazy lovemaking?"

He laughed again and said jokingly: "Madam, was my follies pleasing or substandard? Or, how would you relay this to the Queen?"

She laughed frenziedly and said scandalously, and mockingly: "In order for me to assess your performance and report back to her Majesty, you will have to perform an encore, darling!"

He continued laughing and responded friskily: "Interesting my Lady! I cannot entertain the thought that I will be seen as a jester in her Majesty's palace if my Lady sees my extreme follies as substandard! Can I start the encore right now, darling?"

Elizabeth fell out laughing uncontrollably and replied tawdrily: "Then, my Lord, I will be seen also as a jester in the Queen's palace because I gave my heart to a jester who was incapable of becoming extreme in his follies! That will not bode well for both us of my, Lord! Therefore, I propose that for the next ten days you will have to do encore of extreme follies at least three times a day in order for me to report back to the Queen that you were graded above and super-standard!"

Lloyd continued to laugh irrepressible for a while. Then, he said obscenely: "Madam, your proposal is accepted! And, please be fair in your grading system and judgment!"

She laughed and said lovingly: "I love you, Lloyd! You have already been graded and you passed in flying colors! Now, I am hungry. Let's go upfront and get something to eat!"

Lloyd answered and said tenderly: "I love you too, Elizabeth!"

Then, they both went to the front of the Jet and sat in the sitting area where the hostesses brought them all types and varieties of cuisine plus wine.

It was already early Sunday morning and as they kept eating, they were looking through the window of their cabin and saw night lights as they flew across various cities. Then, they went back to their bedroom and laid down and fell asleep.

Elizabeth woke up at about 10.30 am, London time, naked on the bed and said: "Where are we Lloyd?"

He was also still naked and answered his wife and said: "While we were sleeping, I think we landed in New Delhi and fueled up. We are now heading towards Bali Island. We should be there possibly in about two hours."

She said: "Great! I can't wait to explore the beach and the Island!"

He responded and said: "Me too, darling!"

Then, he got close to her and started rubbing on her behind with his manhood as his hands were kneading her nipples. Craving and longing weld up in both of them and they made love again for over one hour. Lord Astor realizes that his appetite for sex was equally matched by Elizabeth's appetite for sex also. They got up and took showers and came back to bed.

She said anxiously: "I only packed some few clothes to wear! But, nothing for the beach or for Island wears!"

Lloyd said calmly, and wickedly: "Do not worry about that my Lady. There are lot of boutiques and designer shops in Bali where we can buy beach wears and Island clothes. Besides, you may not need any clothes since you will be naked most of the time!"

She laughed irrepressibly and said lasciviously: "Seriously! You mean it is your intention to keep me in our cabin and naked so that you can make love to me all day? Wow! My Lord, that is way too extreme for what I bargained for!"

He laughed uncontrollably and said playfully: "I thought that was your proposal which we agreed on! You cannot back out now of this agreement!"

They both laughed frenziedly!

He continued and said warmly: "Darling, we will be landing soon. Let's get dressed so that we can eat some breakfast and be ready to go through Customs and Immigration Control before being whisked away by our Limousine to our private Island."

She said lovingly: "Ok, darling. Besides, I am starved. I will be quick so that I can eat my meal unhurriedly and be able to see the beauty of the city as we are landing!"

They went to the front of the aircraft and sat in the sitting area as they were being served breakfast.

They finished eating breakfast and watched as the plane landed in Bali in a private airport. They exchanged pleasantries with the Captain and the Crew as they disembark the Jet. Some members of the private Island hotel, including special security and bodyguards, were there to see them through Custom and Immigration. Then, they were put into a limousine and driven to a very private Island within Bali Island. As they were being driven, they saw the beauty of the Island including the flowers, the palm trees, other shrubs, the beaches, the clear blue water and the unique buildings.

They got to their private Island and were checked into one of the largest and luxurious beach cabins they have ever seen. It comprised of three ensuite master bedrooms, two living rooms, two dining areas, and an expansive kitchen and bar area. There was also an expansive patio facing the beach and ocean. They could see the beach and ocean from every room. And, there was no cabin close to where their cabin was located. Essentially, they had great privacy. The waiters and security personnel could only access the cabin through a long gated driveway.

As they got into the cabin and dismissed the waiters and security personnel, Elizabeth head towards the bedroom to drop her bags in the closet. As she got into the bedroom, Lloyd started chasing her playfully in the room as she kept running away from him. He finally cornered her on one side of the bed. He started kissing her passionately and started pulling her traveling clothes off, and at the same time, pulls his clothes off.

She laughed and said erotically: "My husband, this must be your blueprint for honeymoon! In the script, your intention is to incessantly hump me every hour!"

He answered lewdly: "Darling, that is the script!"

He put his hands between her two naked thighs and pulled them apart gently. Then, he entered into her forcefully. She moaned loudly and was shaking deliriously with pleasure. He started pounding into her as his own body was shaking with pleasure. After about twenty minutes, he pulled out of her and sat down with his back to the head board and carried her so that she can sit on him as he penetrated her again. She started moving up and down on him as he thrust upward periodically. They maintained this rhythm for another forty minutes until they both climaxed together. She got up off him and lay by him as he held her close to himself. They were spent and fell asleep immediately.

They woke up at about 2.00pm London's time which was 10.00pm Bali's time. They took a shower, put on their pajamas and got back in bed.

He asked her: "Are you hungry?"

She said: "Yes. I am famished. Are you?"

He replied: "Yes. I am famished too!"

She responded and said: "Please, order dinner, even though it is late!"

He said: "Ok."

He ordered dinner and moved closed to her and started playing with her again, but, she pushed him off.

She said provocatively: "Husband, I am hungry. Please let me be!"

He responded playfully: "Ok. I am just trying to pleasure my wife!"

She laughed and responded mischievously: "Lloyd, did I marry an insatiable freak? I will put you on notice that I can only be humped three times a day and not every hour!"

He laughed frenziedly and responded friskily: "Yes, you did! And, you love this insatiable freak!"

They both laughed uncontrollably!

Their dinner was delivered and they ate their meals.

Then, he started playing with her again and she became extremely wet again as he pulled the bottom of her pajamas off and took his own pajamas off. He pulled her close to himself and slightly raised her right leg as he penetrated her from the side. At the same time, his hands were manipulating her breasts and nipples which became extremely firm. Elizabeth started moaning loudly again as he increased the rhythm of the penetration. They continue to lay side by side as he kept making love to her. Both of their body started shaking in pulsating pattern as they enjoyed orgasmic pleasure. After about forty minutes, they climaxed together as their bodies were shaking intoxicatingly in orgasmic ecstasy. He pulled out of her and continued to hold her in his hands as they fell asleep.

They slept throughout the night. They woke up at about 8.30am Bali's time on a Tuesday morning. .

Elizabeth opened her eyes and said spicily: "What is the plan? Are we engaging in marathon sex, my love?"

Lloyd said iniquitously: "Yes. I thought that is what you agreed to, madam! To be humped as many times as possible so that my extreme follies will be graded excellently!"

They both laughed irrepressibly. She got up and said tawdrily: "Get off of me, Lord Astor! I am going to take a shower so that I can explore the Island and its beaches with you."

Lord Astor said agreeably: "Ok, darling. I am going to join you in the shower. Then, we should go and explore the Island."

She said: "Ok."

They finished taking their showers and put on some casual clothing. Then, they were accompanied by their security personnel as they went to explore the Island and its beaches. As they were enjoying their outings, they kept conversing and discussing their plans for the future as husband and wife.

www.ingramcontent.com/pod-product-compliance
Lightning Source LLC
Chambersburg PA
CBHW060226100726
47907CB00003B/528